AF897661

THE DUKE'S GOLDEN RINGS

FIFTH DAY OF CHRISTMAS

ANNA ST. CLAIRE

Sassy Romances

COPYRIGHT

Copyright © 2020 by Anna St. Claire

All rights reserved.

Cover Design by Teresa Spreckelmeyer

Edited by Jessica Cale, Safeword Author Services

This novel is entirely a work of fiction. The names, characters and incidents portrayed in it are the work of the author's imagination. Any resemblance to actual persons, living or dead, events or localities is entirely coincidental. No part of this book may be reproduced in any form or by any electronic or mechanical means, including information storage and retrieval systems, without written permission from the author, except for the use of brief quotations in a book review.

DEDICATION

This book is dedicated to my husband, who reminds me every day what true love is. It is not roses, chocolates, diamonds or riches. It is that special person that makes a sunny day brighter, a rainy day not so glum, and a pandemic quarantine not so lonely—as long as we have each other.

PROLOGUE

Hampstead Heath, London, England
1 April 1815

Four horses huddled together beneath the heavy boughs of a large elm tree in the early dawn. Cool rain fell gently, producing a layer of fog that sat just above the ground, creating an eerie visage. Four men stood in pairs at opposite sides of the wide tree, taking advantage of the cover the branches offered.

A short round man stepped out of a black unmarked carriage drawn close to the elm.

"Thank you for coming, Doctor Bernard," a tall blond man acknowledged the practitioner, pulling a handful of white cloths from his pocket. "I am Lord Willington, Lord Greystone's second."

After shaking the doctor's proffered hand, Willington strode from under the cover of the trees. He approached one man from the other pair and went about setting up the square. The two men stepped off twenty paces from opposing corners, dropping white handkerchiefs at the established corners. The men then divided into two small groups at opposing sides of the tree. Lord Adam Hunter, Marquess of Greystone, stood with his friend Benjamin Crewe, Lord Willington. Lord Aster stood with his second, Lord FitzRoy, on the farthest end.

"Are you sure you can issue no apology, Lord Aster?" The stout doctor held up his hands plaintively from the other side of the tree.

"I have nothing to apologize for, so no," the man replied, nervously twirling the ends of his long mustache.

"Then I should speak with your second." The doctor returned after a moment of contemplation, then stumbled over to the man's second to discuss the proceedings.

"It is time," Willington announced, tucking a gold pocket watch back into his waistcoat.

"Yes. Thank you, Willington. It *is* time." Adam's voice sounded hard, even to himself. He unwrapped a long box covered in a large oiled cloth and extended it to his opponent. It contained the swords he had inherited from his late uncle. "Choose your weapon, Lord Aster."

God help him, but the man would feel the sting of whichever rapier he did not choose. It had come to this. Honora was dead, and every nerve in his body told him that this man was the reason for her death.

He had survived Waterloo only to return home to find himself jilted by the woman he had professed to love. They had been affianced for months, having signed the documents and discussed wedding plans several times, even in letters. Had Napoleon not reemerged, they would have married by now, and he would have felt blessed to have her by his side as his marchioness.

Honora was dead, having cast herself from a cliff shortly after marrying. His ears had heard of her death, but his head had found it hard to believe. She had been so full of life. His Honora had feared the ocean; he could not visualize her near a cliff, let alone jumping from one.

His heart filled with such pain and anger, he wanted to fight to the death; however, he had agreed to first blood. Aster had chosen swords over pistols, thinking it the safer choice. Adam felt confident with either.

His opponent picked up both swords and examined them, finally deciding on one. Adam gripped the remaining sword from the box, feeling the familiar touch of its hilt in his hand and unexpectedly recalling his father's insistence he have excellent fencing skills—a skill he owed his life to many times over in the war.

The two men walked to opposing corners with swords sheathed. Motionless and quiet, they waited for the signal to start. Lord Willington stepped forward and recited the *Code Duello*, including the agreed upon "to first blood."

"Begin." Willington gave the signal, and both men advanced. The sound of steel clashing and heavy breathing pervaded the grounds for long minutes as each man lunged, parried, and riposted. A moist, heavy smell of sweat added to the wet scent of rain.

Adam knew Aster was tiring. Tension focused him, keeping him alert for whatever his opponent threw. He seized upon the opportunity to draw first blood and nicked Aster on the arm. A river of red seeped through his shirt. Thinking the fight had ended, he turned away.

"Adam!" Willington yelled.

Adam turned, holding his sword prepared to block. He was not fast enough. The tip of Aster's sword had gotten too close and sliced the skin on the side of his face, barely missing his eye. Furious at the breach, he lunged at Aster, burying his sword deep in Aster's side. His opponent went down.

Loud noises of wheels and horses erupted from nowhere, and Adam reeled to see the duke's carriage racing to the scene. "Father," he murmured, barely able to see and scarcely with any voice. Satisfied that his opponent was down, he threw his rapier to the ground and leaned into Willington, allowing him to lead him away from the dueling ground.

The Duke of Lancaster alighted from his carriage and charged into the clearing. "Son!"

They stopped. Wordlessly, his father placed his arm around Adam and pulled him close before he and Willington continued toward their horses. He could hear his father's tone issuing directives, speaking to Aster's second and the doctor.

When they were away, Willington spoke under his breath. "Your father saw Aster's foul play. You were perfectly within bounds—or would be if dueling was still legal. Let us get out of here and let the duke handle things. I believe I just heard Lord FitzRoy affirm to your father that Aster cheated."

An hour later, Doctor Henley, his father's physician, was sewing and bandaging his wounds. Henley was a young doctor who had served in many of the recent battles. He insisted on newer methods of medicine, some he felt strongly about, even though they were not proven. Father liked him. Henley had insisted on cleansing the wound first, contending that it would get any debris out of it. Hell's teeth, the searing pain from flushing the wound hurt as much as the stitches.

"At least your eye remains untouched. You were fortunate, my lord," Henley allowed between stitches. "Our biggest concern will be infection. I will leave instructions and will be back to check on you tomorrow," he said, tightening the thread.

A knock sounded at the door, and his father entered. "Doctor, how is my son?"

The doctor lay down the needle and scrubbed his hands. "I finished closing the wound and counted twenty-five stitches. I made them as small as possible, but your son's face will scar. We will have to wait until healing takes place to see how badly."

"And his eye?" Adam heard his father probe.

"Is safe, for now. I cannot say what will happen if this becomes infected. Try to keep it clean and the bandages changed," the young doctor returned. "I trust that you have taken care of the situation?"

"The other man is in terrible shape," the duke responded. "That is all I know. And Doctor Henley?" He paused. "This *never happened*."

"Understood," Henley responded.

The next day, Adam woke to the news that Lord Aster had died from injuries sustained the day before in a street altercation with no witnesses forthcoming. The assumption would be that it was a robbery that had ended badly.

He tried to feel something—guilt, anger, anything. Reaching his hand to his face, he touched it and winced. He felt nothing—nothing except pain.

CHAPTER 1

Lancashire, England
15 December 1815

A steady snow gently fell from thick, snow-laden clouds as the long funeral procession advanced. His father's friends, all in black, trailed behind him, all except Willington, who walked alongside him. A footman dressed in mourning opened the small gate to the family plot, and the group gathered in the center where a large obelisk stood. Adam stood numb. His father was gone. The man who had always been by his side was being laid to his final rest. His thoughts tumbled to three days before.

"Son, take my ring. You are the duke now. Treat those who serve you with kindness. Be stern in business and take care of your family." The old man gasped, trying to say more.

"Save your strength..." Adam pleaded, gripping his father's hands as if he alone could keep him from leaving.

"It is my time; I had hoped for more. However, you will carry on for me—find love. Loving your mother has always been…" He struggled. "My salvation. *Find love.*" With that, the old duke had taken his last shaky breath.

"Father, do not leave…Father," Adam softly pleaded, squeezing his father's hand as he watched his mother fall over her husband, crying.

"He is gone," Dr. Henley pronounced, leaning over the body and putting his ear to his patient's chest. The doctor started to pull up the sheet.

"No, please let me." Adam held out his hand, stalling the man. Leaning over, he kissed his father and closed the eyes that now held a vacant stare. "I will do as you say, Father."

A loud cough sounded from behind him, riveting his attention back to the funeral.

"In certain hope of the resurrection to eternal life through our Lord Jesus Christ, we commend to Almighty God our brother Edward Hunter, and we commit his body to its resting place…" the vicar droned.

Adam quashed the tears threatening to spill. Father would not want him to be weak with grief—not in front of everyone. *I need privacy, badly*. Had he not just returned home? Father had been the picture of health. How had this happened? His heart failed on the heels of the duel.

Dr. Henley had assured him the duel had not caused it, but Adam could not be sure. Still, there was little he could do now. Aster was dead, and as far as the world knew, he had died defending himself against a thief trying to pinch his purse, a story concocted by FitzRoy. Aster would still live, had he not cheated.

Adam felt emotionless. Tossing the symbolic handful of dirt on his father's grave, he paused, committing it to memory before turning and heading back to the manse. His father had kept the duel quiet, almost as if it never happened. It was something he had not approved of yet never mentioned it again. His only concern was Adam.

The new duke reached up and rubbed a hand over the still ragged scar on his cheek. No one questioned him about the scar, probably assuming it was a war injury. The damned sword had barely missed his eye. The skin had finally healed. The area felt sensationless around it, and the raised, jagged disfigurement was ugly. *I suppose it will be money and not love that finds my duchess.* The mocking thoughts played over and over in his head. He stuffed his hands in his coat pockets and tried to ignore the words of his father. *Find love.*

His mother and sister waited at home for their return. They had prepared a feast to celebrate Father, and then Adam would finally have peace. As he scanned the group ahead of him, he noticed a woman. *Strange. Who could that be?* Tapping his friend, he pointed to the woman standing off to the side of the group.

"Lady Evie Roberts," Willington whispered.

Evie! He had not seen her in years. She had become a beauty. "What is she doing here when all the women are waiting at the house?" Adam hissed, his tone one of irritation rather than concern as he had intended.

"Her father and yours were best friends. I am sure she insisted on coming to pay her godfather respects—a bit of an independent, that one." Willington smirked. "They pulled up in a small carriage and joined the mourners. She did not walk the entire way."

"Thank you," he replied, momentarily embarrassed. "I have not seen her in a long time." He wanted to catch up with her and briefly wondered if she and her father would be at the house after the funeral. "She was friends with Honora…" Adam's voice trailed off.

Honora had not occupied his thoughts as often as she once had after the duel and the nasty business surrounding it had concluded. He had avenged her memory and sought to erase it. She had spurned him, and now love was the last thing he wanted to find. A hideous scar threatened his heart that he would never know love.

"Yes, she has become beautiful in your absence. The duckling has become a swan, as they say," added Willington.

Jealousy shot through Adam at Willington's remarks, unsettling him. Evie and Lord Whitby had remained standing by the side a short distance ahead.

"Lady Evie. Very nice to see you," he managed, stopping to acknowledge them. "My mother and sister await our arrival at the house. Will you join us?"

"Your Grace." She offered a curtsy. "We would love to visit. Your father was always kind and treated me like family," she answered softly.

"My father would not have expected you to come in such conditions," Adam insisted.

"Yes, my heart insisted; however, my hair has rebelled at my perseverance. The snow has dampened my curls." She chuckled. "It will look a fright as it dries—my penance for breaking rules."

Her reference to her hair reminded him of when he had taken Honora and Evie angling. Growing up, he had often taken Evie fishing. On one occasion, a fierce summer storm blew up, forcing them to seek shelter while fishing at a stream a distance from Evie's house. He had noticed a weathered cottage on their way to the fishing hole, hidden beneath heavy vegetation. Without benefit of a brush, Evie's wet locks had dried in disarray, the thick, unruly curls enveloping her head like a helmet. The memory brought a smile to his lips. She had insouciantly borrowed a ribbon from Honora and anchored the mass of hair behind her neck, undaunted.

Her father's somber voice jarred him from his thoughts. "Daughter, we will pay our respects to the duchess before we leave. We should keep the visit short. The storm appears to be worsening."

"Yes, Papa," she returned, giving Adam a side glance. "'Twas nice to see you looking well, Your Grace."

Adam and Willington watched father and daughter climb into the small black carriage parked alongside the road where it met the drive. The driver secured the door to the conveyance, and its horses took off in a brisk walk toward the main house. Adam imagined very few people even noticed; the line of mourners had broken off into small groups.

The number of people that had shown for the funeral surprised him, even though it should not have. His father was known to be both fair and firm. Dread ran down his spine as he wondered whether he could be the man Father had expected Adam to be.

Twenty minutes later, Adam and Willington reached the house. The snow had fallen thick with heavy flakes accumulating on the surfaces. A footman swept the stairs, maintaining spaces for the guests to step.

Servants awaited the guests at the door with hot spiced tea to warm them. Adam was anxious to see his mother and sister and wasted no time in making his way into the parlor. *Too late.* They were already greeting guests. A small receiving line had formed, and his mother and sister stood at the end. A mixture of townsfolk and gentry paid their respects. With the snow, he was sure that they would hurry home, not wishing to be caught in the foul weather.

An hour later, they were saying their goodbyes to those who had lingered to talk, many of Father's business associates and close friends.

"Your Grace, would you have a few moments?" A female voice startled him from behind.

"Lady Evie, I thought you and your father had already gone. We truly appreciate you coming today," Adam said almost mechanically, having said it so often in the last several hours. Discomfited with his tone, he amended himself. "I am glad you came, Evie," he added softly.

"I wanted to welcome you back, Your Grace."

"Thank you." His response still sounded terse, even to him. "I appreciate it. Please forgive my poor manners. These last eight-and-a-half months have been difficult. My father's illness took us by surprise. He was always the picture of health. I had not thought to lose him," he breathed, still trying to apologize with his tone for his earlier brusqueness.

"I think we should take our leave, Your Grace." Evie lifted her head slightly. Spotting her father, she motioned that she was ready to leave.

Adam walked them to the door. "Thank you both for coming." He met her eyes. "Father was very fond of you, Evie." *I was too, yet somehow, I missed that you had grown up.* "You know he would find something to tease you about to make you smile," he added, grinning.

He placed her dark pelisse about her shoulders. His hands brushed her neck, sending twinges of heat through his arms, surprising him. Discomfited, he ambled to a small window in the foyer and watched them get back into their carriage and leave, bewildered at the feelings she had conjured within. He had not given thought to any woman since Honora. Absently, he rubbed his face, feeling the now familiar scar that ran down the side.

"She looked like she had something she wanted to say," Willington said, walking up.

"I thought so too, but she seemed to change her mind. She was a friend of Honora's. I have heard no unkind remark attributed to her," Adam reflected out loud.

"Have you ever spoken to her? Asked her about Honora's decision?" Willington prodded.

"No. I have not. I heard enough when I returned to recognize Aster's hand in her death. Honora must have felt desperate, but we probably will never know more. None of that had to happen."

"I hate all—" Willington started.

"Please, no." Adam raised his hand slightly. "I need to talk about this to someone. If not you, who? I know you have my best interests at heart. The strange thing is, I need some kind of closure. I felt so much rage, and now...only pain over the loss of Father."

"That is not so unusual, Adam, but then, I have never had a serious romance," his friend chided softly.

"It appears I was the only one engaged in that romance," Adam scoffed.

"I am sorry, Adam."

"You are the smart one, Willington, going after the widows," he laughed. "Less entanglement."

"Your father always gave me grief over that." His friend laughed. "He told me to sow the oats and get down to life—that I would be happier."

"Yes, Father and Mother were a love match. I hope that she will be all right with him gone. She has me and my sister, but that cannot be enough." Adam's heart lurched as he recalled his father's final words. "The last thing he told me was to find love."

Both men grew silent.

"All the guests have gone," the Duchess of Lancaster murmured as she walked up from behind them.

"Mother. I did not hear you approach," Adam said before leaning in and giving his mother a kiss on the cheek.

She sighed. "Your father would have been pleased to see so many people. It has been a tiring day." The duchess swiped at a lone tear. "I should go upstairs before I make a cake of myself."

"Nonsense, Mother. Losing Father has shocked us all. It

will be a while before I reconcile myself to becoming the Duke of Lancaster."

"You will make a brilliant duke, son. Your father was confident of that." She brushed the wrinkles from her black parramatta and crepe skirt. "It was nice to see little Evie here with her father. The two men were like brothers." The duchess gave a downcast look, followed by a slight shake of her head. "I will see myself upstairs."

The two men watched his mother make her way up to her room with her maid in tow.

"Your mother is holding up well," Willington said under his breath.

"Yes. It will be a while before she adjusts to Father's absence," Adam said on a sigh. "The weather grows worse outside. I am glad you planned to stay."

As they walked into the wood-paneled room, a footman walked in with clean glasses and a plate of meats and cheeses. "Thank you, Dartmouth. Would you mind making sure that a room is prepared for Lord Willington?"

"Yes, Your Grace."

"I am restless myself and would welcome a glass of scotch. Would you like one?" Adam asked to the nod of Willington.

"This storm is more intense than I originally thought it to be. The skies look like it could snow for days," Willington observed from the window.

Adam opened the corner liquor cabinet and withdrew two glasses and a decanter. He poured two fingers of scotch for both of them, then moved to the tall leather chairs sitting in front of the fireplace. His father and friends had always enjoyed gathering here, and he could understand why. A footman had stoked the fire only minutes before they had come into the room. For a few minutes the men sat silently, watching the embers hiss and pop, sending sparks up the chimney.

"I owe my father a debt of gratitude for taking care of the duel. Yet I was so immersed in my mourning and self-pity, I barely noticed. His patience never waned. I shall always treasure the time we spent together these last months. At least I have that." Adam took a deep sip. "It all seems surreal now."

Willington swirled his drink in the glass. "The duke launched a second search for her body."

"Once I recovered from my injuries, Father filled me in on the investigation. Mr. Palmer, his man of affairs, sent him a missive affirming that Honora's body was never found. They only found her night robe floating in the surf. Considering the strong currents where she met her death, it makes sense," Adam said, his throat suddenly dry. "It just took me a while to accept it. To think that she ended her life, and not understand why had been hard to reconcile."

"Did Palmer question Lady Evie? I know you had wanted to avoid involving her," Willington probed.

"Yes, I still do. As close as she was to my father, if she knew something she would have come forward. Palmer's reports also showed that Lord Aster's pockets were light, and he had counted on Honora's dowry to freshen his coffers. He had not, however, counted on the lady's father's refusal to award the dowry. There had been no agreement, only a hasty away to Gretna Green." A long moment of silence ensued before Adam continued, "Yet, I may pay Lady Evie a visit."

He had finally begun to accept Honora was gone from his life. Being able to see her buried and at peace would have helped. Knowing the reason *why* would have helped. The mirror constantly reminded him he had not been good enough for her.

Was he hoping for information that could soothe his troubled mind or was there something else about Evie that interested him? Evie's face and honeyed blonde tresses flickered in his mind. He had known her most of his life. Why had she captured his attention *today*? Honora had been dead almost a year and he had mourned her.

Suddenly, the realization hit. He really did not want to know anything further on that chapter of his life. What he wanted to know about was Lady Evie.

CHAPTER 2

"Stop!" Evie grabbed her umbrella and rammed the end into the top of the carriage.

"Good God, child! We are within sight of the house. Why are we stopping?" Her father grabbed his seat as they lurched to a stop.

"A cat! By the road—'tis hurt. I could not leave it so." She grabbed her pelisse and pushed open the door.

"Wait, I will go with you," her father said, quickly following.

They walked through the snow off the roadside until she stopped at a tree. Reaching down, she picked up a small white cat with tortoiseshell markings and a bloodied face. "It has nearly frozen to death, Papa. And she looks to be a mother cat." She looked around. "I wonder where her kittens are, or if they are even alive," she said, gaping as she took in the surrounding landscape.

"Let us remove to the house, daughter. Most likely she came out for food and got hurt. Perhaps another animal attacked her. Her kittens are probably protected in a dead tree or some other shelter. Let us take her back to the house and clean her up. As soon as the storm lets up, we can search the area," her father added. "She may lead us to them. Cats are known to be resourceful. If there are kittens, it is likely she has provided a warm den for them, but her injury prevented her return. We will not wait too long to look for them."

"You are right, Papa," she said, cradling the cat close to her and wrapping her pelisse about it. She adjusted the small animal in the warmth of her coat and trudged back to the coach.

Ten minutes later, Evie walked up the steps and stomped on the portico, shedding the heavy wet snow from her half-boots as the door opened. Her father followed behind her. It was freezing outside, and she found herself worried about the kittens. She should not have ignored Papa's warnings about the poor weather and left her muff at home. The roads had remained decent. Without trees covering them, she hoped the sun would keep them that way. Snow was lovely, but it was confining and not her favorite weather. She would definitely remember her muff when she searched for the kittens.

"My lady, my lord, welcome home. I had some hot tea served in your study, my lord, should you desire some," Winters said.

"Yes, yes." The Earl of Whitby handed his coat to the butler and stomped the snow from his boots. "That sounds wonderful. I would like nothing better." Turning to his daughter, he said, "Once you get the cat settled, can you join me?"

"Yes, Papa," she replied, nodding. "Do I have time to secure the kitty and get out of these wet things? Cook will help me settle the cat, and it should not take me long to change. You will forgive my hair." She chuckled.

"Of course. I have a couple of things we should discuss

while I am thinking of it," her father added before hurrying off to his study.

"I promise to return shortly." Evie lifted the front of her dress enough to keep from tripping on the front of her skirt and raced upstairs. Today had been tiring, and she felt chilled to the bone. She wondered what Papa wanted to tell her. That her father had allowed her to attend the funeral with him had surprised her. She knew it would set tongues wagging afterward.

Uncle Edward, as she had known him, would understand. He would have expected nothing less. Playfully, he had called her his little hoyden, frequently laughing about her willingness to climb trees, fish with her friends, and even ride her horse astride. Evie knew it to be a pet name, as he had never forgotten to bring her a treat when he visited and frequently sent small gifts when he traveled. A lump formed in her throat at the thought that she would no longer see him.

A loud purr reminded her of the warm fur ball she carried. "You are lucky I spotted you," she said with a light chuckle. "I used to have a doll named Chloe. She had brownish-red hair. I think the name fits you. You are sorely in need of some nourishment and attention. Cook will warm some milk for you. Thank goodness your cuts are minor, but gracious, they've made a mess of your face. Perhaps Cook has something for it, as well. You will love her cooking, little one."

Cook helped her clean the injury, and it relieved her that it was only a small gash. Evie bandaged the wound and left her new kitty lapping milk when she hurried upstairs to her room. Hastily, she selected a black chambray day dress with silver embroidery and matching lace and laid it on the bed while she pulled a cord, summoning her maid.

Minutes later, a knock sounded on her door before her maid entered the room. "Welcome back, m'lady. Let me 'elp you from those wet clothes," the short buxom woman offered.

"Thank you, Alice."

"How was the funeral?"

"You were right. My appearance at the graveside will probably be discussed until a better topic arises with the *ton.* However, Uncle Edward was special, and I did not wish for Papa to attend alone."

The older woman gave an affectionate pat on her arm before taking the wet dress and draping it on a chair near the fireplace.

What she wanted was a warm bath. She wished she had time to have one. Maybe later. Evie had promised her father she would be down quickly.

"I laid out my black day dress. However, I think the velvet maroon might be warmer, Alice. I feel so chilled."

"I was just thinking the same thing," the Cornish woman said, grinning. "The damp from a day like today seeps into the bones. Let me plait the sides of yer hair and make a soft chignon in the back. It will be pretty," her maid remarked as she exchanged the black dress for the dark maroon. She reached in her pocket and pulled out a small jar. "I will massage some of this cream into those chafed hands."

"I had not realized how chafed they had gotten. They hurt." Evie rubbed them together gingerly. The maid slipped the maroon dress over her head and pulled the laces, cinching them. Evie stepped into the matching satin slippers and sat, smoothing out the skirt. "Alice, I found an almost frozen cat on the way home. She is in the kitchen with Cook. Would you mind looking in on her? Perhaps you can find a suitable basket we can use as a bed for her."

"I would be 'appy to do that, m'lady."

Once Alice fashioned her hair and saw to her hands, Evie gave her a quick hug and hurried to the door. Turning back, she added, "Thank you!" She felt her hair, pleased that Alice had managed to tame her rebellious curls.

Walking into her father's office, it alarmed her to see her father standing at the window, staring pensively at the snow. It had been snowing for hours. Drifts of snow had formed peaks beneath the window and caused an involuntary shiver as she recalled how cold it had been outside. Papa turned and smiled at her.

"Have a seat," he said, absently indicating one of two chairs sitting in front of the fireplace.

"You look concerned. Did I upset you today, Papa?" Evie peered questioningly at him. She hated to do anything to disappoint her father.

"Other than stand outside at the service?" He turned and grinned widely. "No. You have only made me smile, and I could never complain about that."

"It is so beautiful outside. One forgets how frigid the snow really is. I was glad to get into warmer clothing," she ventured, wondering what he wanted to say to her. It looked serious, judging from his wrinkled brow.

"I should get to the point." He took a deep breath and sat down. "I received an offer for your hand in marriage, and before I respond to it, I need to discuss it with you." His tone became more serious. "Your mama and I wanted you to marry for love; our feeling was that arranged marriages already have one strike against them. As my only daughter..." He stopped and regarded the portrait above the fireplace. It was a portrait of him and Mama. Papa stood behind a chair where her mother sat. At Mama's foot sat a small red-striped kitty named Fireball. Evie remembered the kitten. He had been a wedding gift from Papa and had been around for most of her childhood.

"You always encouraged me to take my time," she said slowly, "where courting was concerned." There had always been one special person, but he had never paid her any attention. His face always came to mind when Papa brought up marriage.

"Yes, I have. And I meant it," he added. "The offer is from Lord Brandon FitzRoy, the Marquess of Cleveland." Her father grew silent for a moment. "I told him I would give him my answer tomorrow. I wanted to speak to you."

"I…I…dislike Lord Cleveland, Father," she stammered. She knew him, although not well. More, she knew *of* him. He had been good friends with Lord Aster, or at least they had always been together at *ton* events. Honora warned she should steer clear of him.

She startled. Evie had not thought of Honora in a while. Normally, any time she interacted with Lord Greystone, she thought of her friend. Curiously, not today. Today her heart had only seen Adam. She worried her lower lip, trying to ignore the pang of guilt she felt. Honora had been her friend.

"Do not stress yourself, Evie. I plan to turn him down. However, I felt an obligation to make his case known. I made a promise to your mother to allow you to decide." He walked to the corner of his desk and leaned against it, locking his gaze with hers. "I should say that he, without provocation, acknowledged that you would get a generous allowance to spend as you please. I just thought that sounded like the man knew you," he added. "I know how you value your sense of independence. I want you to find a man that loves you and does not wish to change you."

Evie gulped. "Thank you, Papa." Lord FitzRoy had offered *that?* Perhaps she had misjudged him.

No. I will heed Honora's warning. Mayhap it was the company FitzRoy kept and his reputed gambling, but Honora had been adamant. Lord Aster had eloped with Honora, thinking she would bring a large dowry. Her friend's reputation had suffered drastically over the whole affair. It bothered her that Honora's father allowed his daughter to suffer so. Now her friend was dead. Honora's parents had left for Italy shortly after her death and closed up their estate, creating quite a stir among the *ton*.

"There is another matter," the earl said, breaking her reverie. Reaching into his drawer, he extracted a sealed letter. "From your Uncle Edward." He placed the letter in her hands and stepped back to give her some privacy.

Evie sat down and stared at the writing on the front. It read, *To My Hoyden*. She read it and looked up at Papa with tears brimming her eyes.

"You read it. Edward could never have had enough children, as far as he was concerned, and he loved you from the day you were born. Once upon a time, we discussed betrothals, but your mother wanted you to decide. She was a force." He smiled for a long moment. "Go ahead." He indicated the letter with a nod of his head.

Evie carefully opened the seal and unfolded the vellum. The duke had dated it a week before his death.

My little Evie,

You have always been like a second daughter to me, and selfishly, I had hoped that one day you and Adam would marry and make that so—even so much as believing that you hold feelings for him. Whatever comes to be, I hope you will consider staying in his life as his friend.

It is my belief that what happened when he came home was more a matter of pride for him than an affair of his heart. Keep this in mind.

A word, little hoyden. When love comes your way, snatch it up and nurture it. You deserve the best. I wish I could be there when it happens. It will.

Much love,
Uncle Edward

Tears flowed down her face. Wordlessly, she passed the note to her father.

Lord Whitby read it and wiped at his own tears. "He loved you." He looked up at her. "Can this be true?" He arched an eyebrow.

"You mean…about Adam?" She glanced away. "Once Honora declared her interest, I had no right. And then they became engaged." She swiped at the tears. "Yes. I have feelings. However, he has never noticed me." It felt strange discussing this with her father, but who else did she have? Her mother and her closest friend were both gone. While she had other friends, none were as close. Telling her father of her feelings felt freeing and right.

She had been honorable, but she still cared *a lot*. The moment he had placed her pelisse around her shoulders following the funeral flashed through her mind. A bolt of heat had traveled through to her toes. He looked startled too. *Should she even entertain such thoughts?*

"Good." Her father displayed a wide smile and said nothing further. Instead, he walked to the brandy decanter and poured a small amount into a glass. "Would you care for one? Your mother occasionally enjoyed a drink with me when the day had gotten beyond our comfort levels," he said, handing the crystal tumbler to her.

Evie had the distinct feeling Papa knew something he was not sharing.

CHAPTER 3

Adam woke the next morning with a headache.

"What the hell?" The sun on the snow was especially bright.

"Very sorry, my lord. You requested I wake you so you could conduct some personal business." Tindal, his valet, pulled open the curtains. "It appears your friend is also an early riser. He is downstairs in the dining room."

"Bloody hell!" He sat up and tried to adjust his eyes to the light. "Since when did he get up early?" he complained. He had planned a quick visit to Whitby Manor to see Evie, telling himself it was to ask her if she knew why Honora changed her mind. However, he knew better. No matter what the reason, it changed nothing. He wanted to see *her*, although he was unsure what motivated his need.

He and Willington had stayed awake too late, catching up on their lives since they had last been together and drinking scotch. Squinting at the window and grumbling to himself about the sun and the time, he swung his legs over the side of his bed and began the business of getting dressed. Perhaps hot coffee would be just the thing. Adam enjoyed tea;

however, the coffee chased away certain *ailments* in the morning.

Twenty minutes later he walked into the dining room and found Willington engaged in a spirited discussion with his sister about house parties. He had forgotten Beatrice and Willington had become so acquainted. However, Willington had spent a good deal of time with his family, especially since his own homecoming.

"I believe grouse hunting cruel and will have none of it," Willington said in a low voice. "I no longer allow the sport, including on my property in Scotland."

"What about the supposed overpopulation of the bird?" Bea persisted. "I always hear that excuse at house parties. Do you sidestep the house parties?"

"Have you just met me? I do not go to them." Willington laughed. "I hate the pressure of house parties."

Adam guffawed. "I have never known you to hunt birds or any animals for sport. However, this conversation has my undivided attention, considering grouse season ended yesterday."

"Lady Satterfield's invitation for a late season house party arrived before I left home, and I merely mentioned it to Lady Beatrice when we spoke of the guests who had been here. The Satterfields were among them, and I found that curious." Willington gave a coy expression. "Lord Satterfield mentioned it yesterday. The conversation devolved into what we hated about house parties. Then the subject of grouse hunting emerged." He laughed.

"I wondered how you got there." Adam smiled, replacing the silver pot on the serving tray. "I had not realized you were so informed on grouse, sister," he added with a chuckle.

"I guess we were having a bit too much fun." Willington chuckled, spearing a kipper. "The food is delicious. I had not realized the extent of my hunger this morning. My compliments to the cook."

"Thank you. Cook takes pride in her work. I will pass along the compliment," Adam said, ladling some eggs and bacon onto his plate. "What are your plans today?"

"Mainly, I plan to be here for you, friend. I am up for anything," Willington offered.

"I have a minor matter that should take only two hours." Adam hoped his friend would not mention the previous evening's conversation about his visiting Evie—*to ask about Honora*. Honora had become a sore subject with his mother, who naturally wanted to forget about the entire sordid affair. However, he wanted to see Evie. Had his abrupt behavior yesterday following the funeral created this need? She had always been a favorite of his, but she had seemed too young for him. *How did I ever think that?*

The sound of swishing skirts proceeded his mother's arrival. "Good morning, Beatrice. Good morning, gentlemen," the duchess said, seating herself next to her son. "Darling, if you have a few minutes, I have something I need to give you."

Adam looked at his mother's red-rimmed eyes. She had not slept well. "Certainly, Mother. Let us enjoy breakfast together, and I will join you in your parlor."

"I would appreciate that," she answered softly. "I confess, I am hungry after the strenuous day yesterday."

He watched a footman bring her a warm plate and fill it for her with her usual breakfast fare. She was a kind woman, and the entire household seemed to envelop her with support in this emotional time. He admired the adoration his mother engendered.

"Your Grace, would you like your chocolate?" Another footman stood at her elbow with a small silver pitcher.

"Yes, Dartmouth. That would be lovely. Thank you."

"How about a game of billiards today?" Willington inquired.

"That sounds like fun. I think the last time we played billiards together, you won. I feel the need to redeem myself. I have an important errand, but I can go in a few hours." He found himself wavering on whether to ask about Honora. *Odd. Even mentioning her name stirs an peculiar emotion.* He thought he had loved her; however, he doubted those feelings now. Love would have been more lasting, for both of us he mused. "Let me meet with Mother first"—he smiled at his mother—"and then I will join you in the game room."

"Perfect." His friend stood. "I will meet you at the billiard table. Come prepared to lose *again*." He chuckled as he departed the room.

A few minutes later, his mother set down her mug of chocolate. "That was delicious," she intoned toward the footman standing near the door. "Son, if you have time now, I should like to speak with you privately." She gestured toward her parlor.

"Certainly, Mother." He stood and walked to his mother's chair, withdrawing it from the table and allowing her to stand.

When they entered the parlor, Adam watched with a curious eye as his mother withdrew a small package from her escritoire and locked it behind her, pocketing the key in her skirt.

"Your father left this for you, Adam. I think the best thing would be to let you sort through it first. I am here to answer questions."

Wordlessly, he accepted the small wrapped package and attached letter, opening the letter first. He broke the wax seal and slowly unfolded the letter, recognizing his father's hand.

Son,

If you are reading this, you are now duke. You will make a splendid duke, one that will garner support and admiration from your people and your peers. Trust your instincts and do what you believe in your heart to be right. That is my last piece of advice on the dukedom.

I must ask you a favor or two. The first is to take care of your mother and your sister. Your mother and I had planned to always be together, and this will be difficult for her, as it would be for me. Allow your sister to make the match her heart wants. I know you will be a good brother.

The second is that you keep an eye on my godchild, Lady Evie Roberts. I had hoped to see her married...but it was not to be. If I were to have a second daughter, I would have wished her to be Evie. Finally, I have included a gift for you to use when you find the woman that lights up your own heart. It is a stack of five unique golden rings bound together as one. This has been in the family for hundreds of years. There are two sets—your mother has the other set.

Both the duchess and the dowager duchess wear the sets until death parts them from the world. Each ring symbolizes the hallmarks in the discovery of genuine love: the moment of first notice, first kiss, when (you) realize she matters, when she says 'yes' to marriage, and finally marriage. Traditionally, they have been used as the wedding ring set. My father gave the set enclosed to my mother, and she wore it until her death.

Find love and do not settle, son. I would have wished for more time with you. Do not spend too much time mourning me. I know you loved me.
I love you, Adam.

Father

Adam stared at the letter for a few minutes before unwrapping the small package. Inside, he found a small blue velvet pouch which contained a small stack of five intricately carved golden bands locked together. He was humbled that he had never realized the meaning of the similar set of rings worn by his mother. It dawned on him that Father had never commented on his engagement to Honora. Perhaps he saw what Adam had not seen and waited. Admiration for his father grew in that moment—something he would not have thought possible.

The duchess cleared her throat. "Your father told me he had never shared the story of the rings with you. You must have questions. I am here if you need me." The duchess absently fingered the intricate stack of rings on her left ring finger. "I have never taken my ring off." She wiped a single tear from the corner of her eye and smiled at her son. "Your father knew you would fulfill your duty to the family, but he felt strongly that you must follow your heart."

"He told me as much, but I knew nothing about this tradition." Adam's eyes misted, and he considered his mother. "I am here for you, Mother. I shall cherish both and endeavor to make you proud."

"You never disappoint, Adam," his mother said, patting his hand gently. "Now, go. Go be with your friend."

Adam tucked his father's letter and gift in his inside pocket and climbed the steps to the game room. Confused and anxious, Adam played billiards while his mind sorted through what he had just received. He would visit Evie later.

CHAPTER 4

"M'lady, will there be anything else?" Alice asked.

"Yes. Have you seen Chloe? I wondered how she was doing."

"Ye've named 'er already. I like that name. *Chloe,"* the maid intoned slowly. "Last I saw the cat, she was in the kitchen. Cook was feeding her milk. She was so hungry. I will go downstairs and check, m'lady."

"No. I am going downstairs and can check on her. Maybe Cook has made some of her wonderful lemon biscuits." Her stomach growled in response to her thought and she giggled.

"As you wish, m'lady," the maid replied. "I think I know of a beautiful basket for Miss Chloe. 'Tis one your mother once used for her cat, if I can find it. I have been puzzling over its whereabouts since you brought the kitty home."

"That would be wonderful, Alice. Thank you." Evie rose from the escritoire in her room, having read and reread the letter from Uncle Edward. *I never realized how well he knew me.* She hid the letter away in a small box in the back of the desk and started for the kitchen.

The clanging of the pans in the kitchen and the sound of

Cook's voice caused her to hasten her steps. The woman was masterful at making sweets, and Evie hoped she was in time for some lemon biscuits. Just thinking of them, she could already smell them.

"Afternoon, m'lady." The tall, graying woman rounded the corner from the pantry. "I bet I know what ye want," Cook said cheerfully.

"I would love to have some of your delicious lemon biscuits if you have any to spare," Evie said, trying to look nonchalant while her insides groaned for the treat.

"Ye know I keep a small stash for ye." She turned to her kitchen helper. "Patty, please grab the small tin on the top shelf in the pantry."

"I will be happy to do that, m'lady." The young girl skittered off to retrieve the tin.

"I had just put them in there fer you." Cook grinned. "They are still warm," she said, handing Evie the container.

Evie scanned the room but did not see Chloe. "Cook, I thought I would find my new cat down here. Have you seen her?"

The cook stopped smiling. "I am sorry, m'lady. The cat ran out an hour ago when I was bringing in some wood. She had some milk and a little meat from last night's meal before she left. Do not worry. She will be back."

"Oh, dear. The weather is brutal." Evie bit back her frustration. "I *have* to find her." She glanced at the hooks by the door and noticed an old coat she had given to one of the kitchen helpers months before. Grabbing it, she threw it on and headed out the door into the snow.

Cook ran to the door. "M'lady, wait! 'Tis a dreadful storm out there."

Evie half-turned and faced her. "I will be back soon. I have to find Chloe."

Running out the door, she realized that she had forgotten

her muff again. Her hands were quickly getting wet and cold, even stuffed in her pockets. *Concentrate. Chloe is probably close to where we found her.* Evie fixed her eyes on the ground, deciding it was easier to see that way. She would not allow the poor cat to be lost after just having found her.

The flakes had become smaller and swirled about her head. The atmosphere thickened with the white stuff, making it more difficult to see. Her house was behind her, and she was sure she was getting closer to where she and Papa had found Chloe. Was she? It looked different covered in snow, and she was no longer sure. Nothing looked familiar. It had been snowing all day, she chastised herself. *Foolish girl! You are looking for a white cat in a snowstorm. You should have gained Papa's help.*

Evie thought she heard something and stopped. "Chloe," she called. She could no longer feel her feet, and her hands were no longer red. They appeared tinged with blue.

"Meow."

Excitement warmed her. The sound was faint, but she was sure it was a cat. Or was it a kitten? Hurrying, she trudged through the thick snow in the sound's direction.

"Meow..."

The cry grew louder. She must be close. Evie stilled and looked around. The kitten's call sounded almost on top of her. She peered around. Spotting movement, she looked up at the tree next to her. Chloe and a kitten huddled together on a low-hanging branch, and another darker-colored kitten was crying, huddled at the base of the tree. The mother cat appeared frantic, trying to rescue one kitten while keeping the other safe. What had driven the kitten up into the tree? *Cats normally do not run up trees unless they are trying to escape something.*

Carefully, Evie lifted the kitten from the snowdrift and tucked it into her pocket, delighting as it nestled deep inside.

She studied the limb in front of her with the cats on it. The branch was not too high. Perhaps standing on her tiptoes, she could reach them both. Carefully, Evie reached up and nudged a small red-striped kitten into her hand, depositing it in her other pocket before reaching for Chloe. Chloe looked relieved. Was she giving human characteristics to her cat? She giggled. "Thank God I have found you. Let us go home."

Satisfied with the rescue effort, Evie cuddled the mother cat in her arms and looked around. Snow had covered her footprints, and she did not recognize anything. She was lost. Swallowing her panic, she squinted and stared at everything slowly, trying to identify *something*.

A quick burst of wind whirled the snow and bent the trees, revealing a thin opening through the branches through which she recognized her mother's summer cabin. Whether Providence or a minor miracle of the season, she would take it. "I see a place to wait out this weather, Chloe," she murmured. "Hold on, kitties."

Evie tightened the hold on her charges and ran. It was more of a slow trot since her feet no longer felt like they belonged to her. She reached the door and turned the handle. At the same time, she heard a pig sound and looked behind her just in time to see a wild boar charging through the brush, coming her way. She frantically rattled the doorknob. To her surprise, the door opened. Not questioning why the door was unlocked, Evie chose to be thankful and stepped in quickly, slamming the door closed behind her. A loud bang on the door told her that the wild pig had charged it. She heard his retreat and braced for the worst. If he charged it again, the door likely would not hold.

Trembling, she squinted into the darkness. "I think I recall we always kept the tinder box on the mantle," she said out loud to herself. It made her feel less alone and curiously, a little braver. Spying the window latches, she hastily opened the shutters on a window near her, giving her some light. She felt around the top of the mantle with her free hand, knocking webs and dirt around while still holding Chloe in her other arm and the kittens in her pockets. *I am freezing.* She felt a box and grabbed it. "Thank God! Let us hope that there is a log or something to burn in the fireplace."

Soon there was a roaring fire in the fireplace, thanks to the wood still stacked there, giving a warm glow as heat poured into the cabin. She looked around. Outside of the extreme dust, nothing seemed different from the last time she had visited with her mother. She had often accompanied her mother here when she painted. Mother had been known for her painting talent. They had framed one of her paintings and hung it in Papa's study.

Spying her mother's small chaise lounge, Evie cautiously moved toward it. Carefully, she lifted the covers and folded them as neatly as she could. A heavy cloud of dust motes persisted and floated through the light provided by the opened window curtain. Removing the kittens from her pockets before taking off her pelisse, she curled up on the chaise, giving a small prayer of thanks that the boar had lost interest. Placing the kittens and mama cat at her feet, she used her pelisse as a cover and finally closed her eyes. *Papa will look for me, I am sure. And I will deserve his wrath when he finds me.*

CHAPTER 5

"How can Lady Evie Roberts be missing?" Adam said, panic clear in his voice. "You mean she is lost in *this?"* He gestured behind him at the thick swirling snow, stepping inside so the butler could close the door from the cold. "It is nearly blizzard conditions out there."

"My lord—I apologize, *Your Grace.* We are all most upset. Lord Whitby was just alerted by her maid and is organizing a search party to find her," Winters said, his own voice faltering.

Heavy booted footsteps sounded in the hall, and both men turned.

"Your Grace! I apologize for my hastiness. My daughter has gone missing in this weather." He grabbed his overcoat, hat, and gloves from Winters. "She took off after her cat—we found the critter yesterday, nearly freezing to death. The cat probably went to rescue her kittens, and Evie went to rescue the cat. Now they are all lost in this"—he gestured wildly—"mess!"

"I would like to help. If we need more men, we can send

word to my house. Willington is there and would help," Adam offered.

"I appreciate the offer, but that may slow us down. I can have the footmen fan out across the property. I am hoping to find her quickly. It is brutal out there. It has been snowing on and off since yesterday and shows no signs of slowing. She took off with an old pelisse she found hanging on a hook in the kitchen. Cook is frantic."

Adam turned to Winters. "Please send word to my estate that Evie is missing. Ask them to search the grounds in case she wanders that far." He turned to Lord Whitby and settled an arm about his shoulders. "We will find her. Are there any nearby shelters or small buildings on the estate?"

"Thank you, Your Grace. I would appreciate your help. She is my life. And there are several buildings beyond the stables. There is a small hunting lodge, but that is on the north end of the estate. I would think too far for her to go. We found the cat on the road leading here, and there are several smaller buildings in that direction—some are accessible by the road, and others are located further into the wooded peripheral areas of the estate. I pray she is in one of them. She is a very resourceful young woman, so I am hopeful," he fretted.

"Please call me Adam. You have known me since I was in leading strings and are like an uncle to me. We will find her." Adam thought for a minute. "I would suggest we saddle up. It could be quicker. My horse had no trouble making it here. The snow is not quite a foot deep."

"Yes, thank you, Adam. That would be better than being on foot. Winters, I think it would be quicker for us to move to the stable and saddle up there."

"I would like to join you, my lord," Winters spoke up.

"Thank you, my good man. We need all the help we can get, but perhaps stay close to the house in case someone returns with news. You would know where to find me. Have a footman cover the front and the others divide up the rest of the property. We will search the southern perimeter first, since it is closest." The earl pulled on his coat and gloves.

Twenty minutes later, a party of six men on horseback fanned out slowly toward the edges of the property. Adam kept an eye open for any sign of the outbuildings. He thought he remembered a building near the place they used to fish; however, it had been a long time since he recalled seeing it. It had been inside a wooded area. He would have to be careful in case snow and ice had covered the stream.

The snow paused, and Adam appreciated the break between the gusts of wind. He could hear Evie's name being called behind him, and with each call, his heart tore a little. He had been thinking of her a lot since the funeral. This was not at all how he had expected to find things when he arrived today. It had been a shocking turn of events. His heart's wish was to find her alive and well.

A vision of her in soft azure, her blonde hair swirling about her face flashed in his mind. That was the Evie he recalled just before he left for Eton. What had happened to him that he had ignored her when he returned? He supposed it had been Honora, who had blossomed into a buxom beauty. Evie was still...well, *Evie.* Her soft gray eyes and lithe figure had changed little. *I made a mistake overlooking my friend. How did that happen?*

Honora had been a year older than Evie, and now that he thought of it, she had been more experienced than most of the young debutantes he had known, although he had ignored it at the time. Evie had barely launched into society; Honora had known what she wanted. *This dissembling of my relationship with Honora does little good. She chose another for whatever reason.* Her reasons might have mattered once, but he found he had begun to care less and less.

Large flakes of snow had begun to fall and a breeze kicked up around him, reminding him he needed to find Evie. His father had always spoken of the girl, hoping to do what, he was never sure. When he had announced his engagement, he recalled his father congratulating him. However, the message had come only from Father's lips. His eyes seemed to say otherwise. Adam had thought little about it then. Mother had said nothing beyond congratulations. Beatrice had said *nothing*. How had he missed these signals? They had never disparaged Honora, but had never really welcomed her joining their family, something he was only realizing now.

An overburdened branch fell to the side of him, breaking up his reverie. Adam peered into the wooded area. He thought he detected a wide area that signaled a path beneath the snow. It would not be out of the realm of possibility that she had come this way. Something inside urged him on. "Evie," he bellowed.

The sound of grunting alarmed him, and he turned. Were there wild boars out here? He remembered that Evie used to jest about him being a boar, but she never mentioned having them on the property. Perhaps the cold weather has pushed them to forage for food.

The grunting got louder. He tapped his pocket, making sure he had remembered his pistol.

"Evie! Are you out here?"

The grunting became louder, and his horse's ears pinned back. It *was* a boar. He urged calm with his mare and turned her to face the source of the sound. It was diagonal from where he was heading. The grunting got closer, and the underbrush moved as a black boar charged at him. His horse reared up, and he pulled his gun. Bouncing around on the saddle made it hard, but he aimed for the head of the animal and shot. The animal stopped in its tracks and fell only a few feet from his horse.

"You did good, girl." He petted her mane, gentling her as she neighed and danced nervously in a circle. Carefully, he slid from his horse and tied her reins to a nearby bush. He felt sure the boar was dead, but he was not taking any chances. Rolling the animal over, he noticed one tusk had broken off. "That is odd," he noted out loud.

"What is odd?"

Adam had been so focused on the dead animal, he missed hearing the earl's horse approach.

"I did not mean to scare you. I heard your gunshot and feared something like this. We have seen boars on the property, but not in a very long time. I thought you were signaling you had found Evie."

Adam looked away. He truly wished he had. *Where was she?* "No. Luckily, it gave me a bit of warning. Grace, here, acquitted herself admirably," he added, patting the mare's neck. "Let me show you something." He walked back to the boar and squatted down on his haunches. "He has broken a tusk. It looks like a fresh cut."

"That is odd. I cannot imagine the animal rammed a tree. And to have only lost one tusk," the earl added, his face showing signs of weariness and worry.

"We will find her, Lord Whitby. I was just heading to where I used to take Evie and her friends to fish. I recalled a small cabin we found once when we were caught in a storm."

"That would be the cabin that her mother used to refer to as her sanctuary. It is off to the right of the small stream that runs through the forested area of the property. Follow me."

The earl took off at a faster pace. Adam pulled himself back into the saddle. "Let's go, Grace." The brown bay took off in a faster trot as if sensing the urgency—that, or she wanted to get away from the dead animal.

Branches along the path hung low, making it obvious no one had used this path in years. Clearing the trees, Adam smelled smoke. He glanced over and saw Evie's father had also noticed. "There is smoke rising above the trees near the stream." His heart quickened. "Perhaps it's that old cabin." Excitement rose in his throat.

Lord Whitby nodded. "My wife's cabin! She has to be there."

The two men urged their mounts on quickly.

CHAPTER 6

A loud shot woke Evie from a dream. She had finally gotten warm. "What was that?" she screamed, bolting upright. It took several moments to recall where she was and how she had gotten there. *Was that a gunshot?*

Glancing around, she saw no signs that the noise had affected anyone. *Did I dream it?* She glimpsed the end of the chaise. Chloe and her two kittens were snoozing. Contented, Chloe opened one eye and looked at Evie, then pushed her front paws forward, stretching. "You have to be hungry, girl. I wish I could offer you something, but we are stuck here until Papa finds us. He will find us," she said as a tacit assurance to herself. She had been dreaming of Adam finding her. In her dream, he had come looking for her and had wrestled a wild boar on his way. He had just burst in, sword in hand, ready to slay any other dangerous dragons—and then the shot sounded, waking her. She snorted at the ridiculousness of it. *A woman could dream, could she not?* She felt sure he would never notice her.

"Oh, Uncle Edward! I wish you were right. 'Tis almost Christmastide. It would be wonderful if Adam felt for me the way I do for him." She shook her head and stood. The floor was cold. Quickly, she reached for her stockings and shoes, having placed them near the fire to dry. She had just gotten the second shoe tied when she heard horses.

Peering out the window, she could not believe what she saw. Adam and her father were both riding toward her—or at least it looked like Adam. *I need to stop thinking of him as Adam. He is His Grace now,* she chided herself absently. Excited, she ran to the door and opened it at the same moment her father was reaching for the handle.

"Evie!" The earl grabbed her and pulled her close. "I was so worried! What possessed you to leave the house like that? You almost worried me into my grave."

"Papa, I am sorry," she said, her voice full of contrition. "I should have found you, but you might have tried to talk me out of looking for Chloe, and I was worried." She turned back and pointed at the cat who had stood and was still stretching with two small kittens still nursing, dangling from her. Evie chuckled. "I think they were starving." She turned back to her father and looked past him to Adam.

"Adam! Your Grace, you came. Thank you." She shook her head, trying to abate the sudden rush of embarrassment. How had she fouled up a simple note of appreciation? She recalled her dream. "How awkward. I apologize."

"Nonsense. I was calling on you and found you gone. Of course I would help find you. My father would have never forgiven me if something had happened to you," he said, laughing.

"Thank you for coming." She walked behind them and looked at the outside of the door. "We barely made it in here before that happened," she said, pointing at the damage.

Her father walked to the door and pulled out the broken tusk. "This must be the same boar you just killed."

"You killed a *boar?"* She giggled. Oh no! Had she just

giggled at something so serious? *Nerves.* A blush heated her neck. Adam has always had that effect on her.

"Yes. However, I cannot understand the amusement. I would have expected horror or something, but not laughter," he said with a glimmer of humor in his eyes. "Then again, I have never expected normalcy from you, Evie," he added gently.

"'Tis just that…" She hesitated. *Should I tell him?* Nibbling her lower lip, she continued, "In a dream I had just before you arrived, you killed a boar." She watched his face.

"What happened in your dream?" he inquired in a low voice.

"It was very strange," she hedged, deciding it was best to not answer directly, lest she risk sounding crazy. She turned to her father. "I have never seen a wild boar before, Papa, although I recognized the danger as soon as I heard him. Do you think there could be others?" An icy shiver escaped her.

"I have seen them, although it has been a long time. I used to warn your mother of their existence." He gave a wistful sigh. "She never believed me but always brought her small handgun with her when she visited this cabin to humor me. Your mother was a crack shot, in case you were not aware." He smiled. "I never minded her going as long as she took her pistol. And she never spotted one."

"Yes, well, we had one today. Looked to be a male. Perhaps there are no more," Adam added, arching his brow slightly. "I am relieved you are safe. Can I offer you and your…brood"—a smile creased his face—"a lift back to the house? I see a good-sized basket over there." He pointed to her mother's old knitting basket.

Her father nodded, approving of Adam's offer. "I shall transport Chloe and her babies back. Cook is going to shame us soundly when she sees this many cats." He chortled.

"Nonsense, Papa. The new mousers will thrill her!"

They all laughed at the thought of Cook and a kitchen full of felines.

"Daughter, you scared me soundly. I thought I had lost you." The earl's face became serious as he walked to Evie and hugged her close. "Promise me you will never take off in such weather again."

Pushing back the tears that threatened, Evie nodded, burying her face in her father's chest. "I love you, Papa. I promise never to cause you such worry again. And thank you too, Adam." She wondered if he minded being called Adam. That is what she had always called him growing up. *Your Grace* seemed too formal for the man who had taught her to fish and swim as a child.

"You are welcome. I would still ask that you favor me with a visit if you are feeling up to it."

"Yes, if you will allow me time to change when we get back to the house."

"Of course," he allowed, pinning her with a gaze.

"What should we do with the boar?" her father interrupted. "It would be a shame to leave it behind. It would make a wonderful addition to our Christmastide celebration. And I know Cook will know just how to take care of the meat until then," her father interrupted their attentions on each other.

"Splendid! Boar meat has a rich, nutty flavor and would be an excellent choice for a feast," Adam added.

"Perfect. You will attend our celebration and include your mother and Lady Beatrice as well?" The earl was persistent.

There was a strange gleam to her father's eyes that Evie tried to ignore. *Was he attempting to matchmake?* She had admitted to feelings for Adam when she had read Uncle Edward's letter. Maybe that had not been a good idea. She was sure Adam felt only friendship for her. He had not even noticed her when he chose Honora.

Papa picked up Mother's old basket and placed the kittens and mother cat inside, latching it. "Just until we get home, Chloe. We do not need another adventure so soon." He chuckled, securing the basket in front of him on the horse.

Adam looked to her father as if to ask permission to carry her on his horse. Evie noticed Papa's slight nod. Minutes later, after banking the fire in the fireplace, they left the cabin and were off toward the house.

Three men on horseback were riding in their direction.

"The footmen. They covered the estate on horse and foot to help find you," her father offered, acknowledging them. "What great timing."

The horses slowed and pulled up alongside the earl's horse.

"Thank goodness you found her, my lord. We found no sign of her anywhere, and with the daylight fading, we had become concerned. Then, we heard a shot near us, and rode in the direction, hoping it was a sign that you had found Lady Evie," Dartmouth explained.

"I shot a boar that appeared out of nowhere and charged me and my horse. I had no choice," Adam explained. "Meanwhile, Lady Evie was holed up, safe in her mother's art cottage."

"We appreciate all of your efforts, men," the earl added. "Dartmouth, perhaps you can figure out how to secure the boar. You will find it around that bend," he said, pointing at the path they had just taken out of the wooded area.

"Yes, my lord. We shall see it done," the footman responded enthusiastically as the three men left to locate the dead boar.

Adam clutched her a little closer to his body, hoping to keep her warm. "Let us get you to Whitby Manor and into warmer clothing," he said softly. With the house in sight, he nudged his horse to go faster. He could already see Winters descending the steps.

~

It relieved Adam to have found Evie. The charging boar had startled him, making it more imperative they found her quickly. Thankfully, it had been only one, and she had been safe. When he picked her up and placed her on the horse, a jolt of awareness shot through his body, catching him unawares. Her closeness had stirred his heart with feelings that he thought he might not have again. He leaned a little closer, taking in the rich scent of roses in her hair. Before he could comment, her father rode up beside him.

"I will take our cat family in through the kitchen, so I can turn them over to Cook's ministrations. The footmen should be back soon with the boar. Cook will be thrilled," he said jovially, relief evident on his face. "You two go around to the front, if you will. I suspect that is where most of the staff will look for her return."

"Thank you, Papa," Evie responded.

Adam nodded and brought his horse around, headed to the front of the house. He spotted Dartmouth and the others returning and instinctively shifted in his seat, giving a little more room between him and Evie for propriety's sake.

Evie swung her head around and looked at him. "Thank you for coming to my aid. I had not meant to create such a stir." She looked embarrassed.

Interesting choice of words. Indeed, she stirred something he had never felt before. "I arrived as everyone had just discovered you missing and insisted on being part of the search party," he explained. "Rescuing little Evie will never grow old." He touched her chin affectionately, then pulled back his hand, suddenly recognizing the overt familiarity.

"You mentioned wanting to see me. Can you wait until I change? Perhaps warm yourself in father's study, and I will join you there?"

"I will do that." He looked ahead for a moment. They were almost at the front of the house. "Are you sure you want me and my family descending upon yours for the holiday? I can make up an excuse..." He rubbed his face, feeling the scarred skin, suddenly feeling self-conscious.

"Nonsense! Of course we do. We are friends. You have had so much more going on these past months." She reached up and ran her fingertip along his scar. "Does it hurt?"

He watched her face, waiting for her to recoil, but it did not happen. "Some. It is healing."

"It adds something—a ruggedness." She nibbled her lower lip. "I should apologize for that, but I cannot."

He hooted with laughter, as much from the relief of finding her as from the awareness she was not repulsed. "Never apologize, Evie. Your honesty is refreshing."

"Papa and I would love to have you—your entire family—join us next week for Christmas dinner. Cook will delight in preparing a meal for more than just us." Evie smiled up at him.

Never had he noticed her beauty as much as he did in that moment. Her gentleness and unselfishness shone in her eyes. He could see Evie's heart in her smile. How had he never noticed? He realized he felt more than attraction. Thinking her missing in this storm had him panicked beyond reason. He had always had feelings for Evie. But what were they now, exactly?

Winters and a footman descended the steps of the house in a rush as they approached. He noticed the older man brush something away from his eyes. Tears. This woman had the affection of the household, just as she had captured his father's heart.

"Thank God you found her, Your Grace," Winters effused as he stood near the bottom of the steps, allowing the footman to take the reins of the horse.

Adam dismounted and turned to receive Evie. She pulled her pelisse tighter and slid down. A wave of awareness shot through him again. On impulse, he squeezed her hand, and she smiled up at him.

He cleared his throat. "She found shelter, Winters, and we probably owe a debt of gratitude to a wild boar," he said, winking at her before turning to the butler and following him into the house.

"We have had some problems over the years with a couple of larger ones," the older man said, nodding. "Your Grace, Lord Whitby is in his study and asked that you join him. Lady Evie, welcome home." The relief was clear in the older man's voice. "Your father ordered a hot bath for you," he added.

"Thank you, Winters," she answered.

Winters removed her pelisse and checked the pockets. "My lady, you had no gloves...again," he said, chastisement in his voice.

"I guess it would not help to tell you that I had not planned to leave." She smirked.

"No, m'lady, it would not. Your hands are raw." He nodded pointedly at her hands before reaching for Adam's coat and hat.

"Apparently, leaving without dressing for the weather properly is a habit with you, Lady Evie," Adam observed, warmed by the obvious affection Winters held for Evie.

She winced. "I left my muff home when I accompanied Papa to Uncle Edward's funeral," she admitted. "But I endeavor to do better." With a quick smile, she squeezed the older man's hand and hastened upstairs.

"I apologize for my apparent forwardness, Your Grace," Winters said with a sheepish smile.

"Nonsense. You have been part of this family since before she was born. Lady Evie creates a desire in others to nurture."

"Thank you, Your Grace," the retainer said, reassured.

"Ah, there you are, Adam." The earl turned from the fireplace, wearing a smile as Adam entered his study. "I was enjoying a brandy. I think we deserve one after the afternoon shared."

"That would be perfect, my lord," Adam quipped.

"Please, call me Franklin. I can never replace your father, but if you need me for anything—if I can ever help you with anything—please call on me. Your father and I discussed much over the years. As you know, we did everything together—hunting, family trips, even Parliament. He was my friend for as long as I can remember..." His voice trailed off. "I shall miss him. However, he would want us to celebrate his life, not mourn his death," he said, holding his glass out for a toast.

There was a moment of quiet. "Yes, I believe you are right," Adam finally answered, clinking his glass with his host.

"I do not mince words, son. My daughter cares for you. And she will not forgive me if she finds that I told you this. I trust you will tread carefully where her heart is concerned."

Surprised, Adam coughed. "Just like Father, straight to the point," he choked out.

"I love my daughter," he replied. "The two of you have always been friends. And I suspect more could come of it," he said. "That is all."

Why did he feel like his father was in this room, watching him with a cheeky smile?

"Franklin, I assure you that I will treat Evie with the

utmost care. For the first time in many months, I feel alive around someone and not feeling sorry for myself. With your permission, I would like to see more of Evie if she is interested."

The earl sipped his glass, slowly studying Adam. "You need to forgive yourself, son. You are blameless—"

"How can you say that? I killed a man."

"A man who cheated," the earl finished.

"Does Evie know about the duel?" Adam asked, concerned.

"No. She knows only of Honora's death. It is something you will both need to address before she hears from someone else. Edward did all he could to keep it quiet, but with his death, the assurances may have...weakened. I suggest you tell her."

When she touched his face, he had wondered if she knew of the duel. "You make a good point, Franklin. I will take care of that before she is hurt."

"Your father had gotten a statement written by FitzRoy and witnessed by the attending physician in case anything came of this. He asked me to tell you."

Adam could only nod.

Rustling skirts caught his attention as Evie came into the room. "Papa, thank you for the warm bath. I had not realized how chilled I was." She glanced at her father before pinning her gaze on Adam. She walked over to the fireplace and held her hands over the fire. "I am afraid that my hands will never warm. Winters has made it his personal mission to see that I dress warmly, and he was most distressed to learn I had slipped outside without gloves."

"Yes, he cares. Perhaps he has suffered frostbite before and worries about it happening to you. He is a good man," he said, drawing his daughter close for a kiss on the cheek. "Ahem. Well, if you two can excuse me, I need to check on what has become of the boar," he said, placing his empty glass on his desk before leaving the room. The door remained open.

"You look warm and refreshed," Adam observed. He felt a powerful urge to pull her close. "If the weather subsides, I was thinking you might enjoy a sleigh ride tomorrow." The words blurted from his lips. Had he just asked to court her? He should mourn his father, yet he knew his father would approve. Willington planned to leave tomorrow and get back to his family, so there would be no other limitations on his time. He craved this feeling of life he had around her and wanted more.

"I would love to," she intoned, a look of curious wonder in her eyes. "It has been a long time since I have ridden in a sleigh."

"I stumbled upon the sleigh in our stable the other day. I recall that Mother and Father used it the rare times that we had enough snow." He moved his head, gesturing at the window behind him. "I think this qualifies," he said in a near whisper. He hated to wish his friend on his journey, but he felt inexplicably drawn to Evie. "Will tomorrow be too soon?" he asked, his voice almost trancelike.

"I am sure that Papa would approve," she said in animated tones with her pert nose turned up to him. "And I shall endeavor to meet Winters's approval." A short giggle escaped.

"I shall call on your tomorrow at ten," he said, taking her hand and kissing it. "And I shall bring a surprise."

"Tomorrow cannot arrive soon enough," she murmured as he reached the door.

Adam left wearing a smile.

CHAPTER 7

The next morning, Evie woke before Alice opened her door.

"Good morning! This will be a good day for you, m'lady! Here is your chocolate," she said, placing the small oval tray on the table next to Evie. "And this came for you this morning." She extracted a letter from her pocket. "'Tis a mess. It looks like it had been buried before it was mailed." The cockney maid tutted and shook her head.

A letter? When was the last time she had gotten one? "Perhaps I should read it with my chocolate." She took the letter and settled against her pillows. "Thank you, Alice."

"Mind you wash your hands after handling that. I plan to wash my own, as well," she fussed before leaving.

The handwriting looked familiar. The outside of the letter looked like it had been in the mud. Yet she could still make out the letters. A cold feeling inched its way up her back. The writing resembled Honora's.

Evie sat up suddenly, nearly choking on a gasp. How could this be? Her friend had been dead almost a year now. Was she being punished for realizing her chance at happiness? Taking a deep breath and bracing herself, she carefully opened the missive. The writing was a little smudged inside. Perhaps Alice was right. The thing looked like it had lain in a mud puddle. She wondered if Winters had asked the messenger about its condition. She would ask.

1 February 1815

Dearest Evie,

Lord Aster is not the man I thought him to be. I find myself with child and married to a man who resents my very presence. If only Father had honored my dowry, things may have been different. Yet I would never have known the man that I married. He is cold-hearted and not what I thought.

Once, I had everything I could have ever wanted in life and tossed it away for a man that I loved. My real regret is hurting Adam. He never deserved to be treated with such callous treachery. When you see him, please tell him that I am sorry. I made so many mistakes, but hurting Adam was my biggest.

You have been my kindest friend and never deserved to have a friend like me, who would pursue the man she knew to hold your heart. Please accept my apologies, dearest Evie. I am truly sorry. Life has a way of repaying you for your sins, and it seems that I am becoming acquainted with retribution.

I will never see you again. But you deserved an apology and an explanation. You deserve all the happiness life offers. Please take care of Adam...and tell him I am sorry. He deserved better.

Your eternal friend,
et cetera,

Honora

Evie buried her head in her pillow. It was as if the letter had come from the grave. Adam was due to arrive any minute. What should she do? She felt like he needed to see this. Looking up, she tugged on the rope.

Alice knocked softly and opened the door. "Yes, m'lady?"

"Alice, can you ask Papa to visit me?"

The older woman gave her a look of concern but nodded and left to locate the earl.

A few moments later, she heard his knock.

"Come in," she answered.

"Evie, is everything all right?" Her father walked in the room with concern etched on his face.

"I have something I want to share with you, Papa."

He arched a brow. "Now that is serious."

"I received this." She handed him the letter and watched him open it.

His eyes widened. "This is from Honora. It appears to be a note that substantiates her jumping to her death. It appears she wanted to make known her reasons."

"It does, Papa. I do not know how to handle this. I need your guidance." She swiped a rogue tear from the corners of her eyes. "She knew. She knew I cared for Adam, yet she pursued him and broke his heart."

Her father sat on the bed and pulled her closer, kissing the top of her head. "Sweeting, I believe you will do the right thing." He took a deep breath.

"I know, Papa. It hurts on so many fronts. I thought by not speaking up, I was being good to one friend, and because of that, I lost another friend—at least I thought I had. Now it seems that Honora is gone for good."

"Did you know she was pregnant?" he asked quietly.

She looked away. "I suspected as much. She was

increasing before she married. We never spoke of it, yet I believe she realized I knew."

"How sad for her parents."

"Papa, does it sound awful to say that the letter makes me feel better about spending time with Adam?"

"Your friend died almost ten months ago, and she married another. I know you cared for her, but you must live your life, daughter."

She sighed. "Thank you. I appreciate your guidance, Papa. I think I needed to talk about it. I must get ready. Adam will be here soon."

"You will know the right time to show it to Adam. Nothing in that letter changes anything he has not known or has not realized by now. *Remember that,*" he emphasized. The earl stood up. "I shall see you downstairs. And I will speak to Winters and see if the messenger said anything else when he left the note," he said before he closed the door behind him.

As soon as her father left, Alice entered. "We must get you ready, m'lady!" she said in excited tones. "His Grace will be here very soon."

She chose a dress of black velour over sarcenet with white lace trim. It matched her black pelisse with white fur trim and black fur muff. Alice pulled her hair up into a loose chignon, leaving curls to softly frame her face.

As soon as Alice tucked in the last curl, Evie shot up, anxious to get the day started.

"M'lady, he 'asn't arrived, yet. Take yer time," Alice chided good-humoredly.

She gripped the doorway, stopping before making it all the way through and facing her maid. "You are right, Alice. My comportment should not involve skidding to a stop at the front door. I will endeavor to move more like a lady," she said, grinning.

"I know you are excited. Off with you," the maid said with a chuckle.

Truthfully, she was nervous. When *should* she talk to Adam about the letter? Before the ride, during, or after? Perhaps Papa was right. She would know the right time.

Evie heard her father questioning Winters about the correspondence as she approached the parlor, and she slowed her advance.

"It arrived looking quite ragged. Did the messenger mention anything that would explain the appearance?" the earl questioned.

"Not much, my lord. I remarked on its appearance, as well. He said it had been pinned on the floor, under the edge of a counter. It seemed a reasonable explanation," Winters supposed.

She smiled at her father and Winters and walked into the parlor at the same time Adam arrived. She heard his brief exchange of niceties with her father before Winters brought him to the parlor.

"These are for you, Evie," he said, holding a small bouquet of white roses and sweeping his eyes over her. "You look lovely."

A pulse fluttered in her throat when his dimpled chin, dark wavy hair, and tawny brown eyes caught her gaze. She blushed when she realized he had stopped talking and was looking for a response. "I am sorry. I was trying to think of how to thank you for the white roses. They are my favorite," she replied. She could not take her eyes away from him.

"I have hot bricks and blankets waiting. Shall we go?" he queried, his eyes twinkling.

Their sleigh ride was nothing short of a fairy tale. The white sleigh, pulled by two white horses, glided its way over roads padded by over a foot of snow, beneath glittering boughs of crystalized leaves. Snuggled under a red velvet blanket with warming bricks at her feet, Evie could not recall when she had seen this much snowfall.

"The horses are beautiful!" she exclaimed. She had never seen such perfectly matched white horses.

"They are Andalusians. I was able to have them transported home from the peninsula. Warfare nearly wiped out the breed. I thought to try my luck at horse breeding and secured permission from Wellington to send them to England. As it happened, they arrived with his horse."

"Have you named them?" she asked.

"No, as a matter of fact, I have not. Would you like to name them?"

"Truly? I have never gotten to name a horse!" she exclaimed. "What do you think of Luna and Legacy?" she asked, nibbling her lower lip.

"I love it," he answered. "Are you warm enough?" Adam asked. "I thought we would make a special stop in town."

The sleigh approached the front of a small confectionary shop and stopped. Within minutes, his footman returned with two mugs of steaming hot chocolate and a bag of small vanilla-iced biscuits.

"I love hot chocolate from this shop and thought you might enjoy it."

"Mmm. I enjoyed a cup this morning. It is my favorite thing to wake up to in the morning."

The small Lancashire village had been filled with people shopping and making their way about, occasionally acknowledging the couple as they moved through the snowy countryside. Evie barely noticed anyone but Adam.

As the sleigh headed back in the direction of her home, Evie felt the compulsion to speak about the letter, reasoning that he might leave when he dropped her off and her opportunity would be gone. She hated marring the beautiful day they were enjoying, despite the pull to do the right thing.

"I have something I need to show you. It just arrived, and..." Her words died as she looked away.

"What is it?"

"I received this when I woke up this morning and have wanted to find the right moment to share it. Unfortunately, there is no perfect time." She raised her eyes and looked at him intently.

"You have my attention."

She felt a nervous tightening in her throat. Evie reached into the deep pocket of her pelisse and withdrew the letter. "It is Honora's hand. The messenger told Winters it had been wedged under something and was overlooked for a time," she offered, placing the letter in his gloved hand.

Adam opened the vellum and began to read while Evie looked away. It would be just her luck to have a hand from the grave snatch away the man she had always wanted.

Adam read the letter. He immediately understood Evie's hesitation at sharing it and appreciated her honesty. Upon reading it, it was as if an invisible yoke of residual anger, pain, or the other myriad emotions that drove him to duel over her had lifted. This letter proved their relationship had *never* been as he had imagined. Honora had wanted another, had loved another and had tragically died. Adam had never spoken with her parents because they had left so suddenly. Honora's letter lifted a cloud he had not realized hung over him. Her letter was a gift.

He turned to face Evie. "I am sorry that Honora's life came to this," he said softly. "For the first time since my return home, there is peace when I say her name."

"I think I understand," she whispered hoarsely.

He studied her face. "You have taught me there is more to the heart than attraction."

"I have?"

"Yes. When we are together, I find that I cannot get enough of you." He laughed, pulling her to him. He smoothed back the hair from her face. "I am doing a bad job of this, but what I am trying to say is, I have developed strong feelings for you, Evie. And this letter"—he held out Honora's note—"this gave me the gift of freedom. Thank you for that."

His eyes focused on her full pink lips.

"May…may I kiss you?" he whispered as he moved closer. He could think of nothing else he wanted or needed at that moment.

"Oh." She blew out a nervous breath. "I…would like that, Adam," she murmured, tilting her head up.

He leaned in and brushed her lips, teasing them open with his tongue. When she opened her mouth, his tongue swooped in and swirled around, caressing and gently memorizing the feel and taste of her. She tasted of chocolate. It immediately became his favorite flavor and would forever remind him of her.

Passion ignited within him. He pressed his mouth into hers with increasing pressure, creating murmurs of pleasure between them. His need to know more of her grew. His lips slid to her face, and he sprinkled her with small kisses, memorizing the shape of her face and the feel of her skin beneath his lips. He gently kissed her closed eyelids and moved down the column of her delicate neck, kissing and nipping. Almost effortlessly, he slid the blanket off her shoulders and unhooked the top of her pelisse as his mouth slid to her exposed décolletage. He could feel his need quicken with his pulse as he kissed the rise of both breasts that moved with her breathing.

Unwilling to push further, he returned to her full lips,

covering them with his, gently nibbling, encouraging her to open her mouth for more. She sighed with pleasure and he seized the opportunity to familiarize himself with the texture and feel of the inside of her mouth, encouraging her tongue to join his, mingling together in a fervid dance of desire. A hunger for her consumed him. His loins stirred and he felt all control begin to leave. Forcing open his eyes, he broke the kiss, eliciting a small gasp from her and leaving them both panting.

Evie gently ran her fingers over her bruised lips and looked up in bewilderment at Adam.

The heat of their kiss had stirred a level of hunger that Adam had never experienced—a passion born of something more than simple need. "I never—"

"Stop," she whispered. Evie reached up and gently cupped his face, her eyes locking with his. "Adam, please do not say you did not mean to kiss me. I have waited for *that* kiss my entire life."

His heart melted. "I was going to say that no kiss has ever stirred such desire and elicited such need. You have captivated me."

CHAPTER 8

Christmas Day

Evie woke to an abrupt entry of sunlight into her room as Alice opened her curtains.

"Good morning, m'lady." She beamed as she bustled around the room, assembling an outfit for her charge. "You have a visitor. The Duke of Lancaster is here to see you."

Evie sat up in the bed. "Adam is here?"

"Yes, m'lady. The duke is in the master's study at the moment," Alice returned.

"He is speaking with Papa?" Evie asked numbly. They had just seen each other—in fact, they had seen each other every day since the day he found her in her mother's cabin a sennight before. Her father had invited his family to celebrate Christmastide tonight. A giggle escaped her.

"I placed your chocolate and toast on the side table," the older woman said, giving a nod to the table beside her and breaking into her thoughts. "And there is warm water in your ewer for your ablutions. I will be back in fifteen minutes and help you dress. You do not want to keep your duke waiting, now do ye?"

Was he her duke? Everything had moved so quickly.Ever since he had taken her for a ride on his sleigh. A beautiful gold and white sleigh. On a sigh, she fell backward onto her pillow and stared up at her ceiling. Could any day have ever been as perfect?

Evie would never forget the dreamlike sleigh ride. She nestled her head further into the down of her pillow and closed her eyes. The days had flown by playing chess, taking walks, and horseback riding. Evie had even helped deliver gift baskets to Adam's tenants the day before.

He had arrived yesterday, holding a bouquet of white roses grown in his hothouse. Evie had received flowers from callers before, but she had never received roses before, let alone such beautiful white ones. The flower had always been a particular fancy of her mother's, who had received them from Papa. There was something special about their fragrance that Evie loved. It made her think of Mother.

A knock sounded, and Alice entered the room. "Lordy, m'lady, ye have a very patient visitor waiting downstairs for ye." Her smile stretched from ear to ear.

"Why are you smiling that way, Alice? Do you know something?" He had spoken to Father. What could that have been about?

"What makes ye sure I know something? The only thing I know is that ye need to hurry up. Look at ye, still in bed," she said, giving her a wink.

Alice helped Evie into her stockings and undergarments. "Ye would look fetching in this deep purple dress," she muttered, guiding the garment over her head and cinching it. The dark purple crepe had a shimmering quality and lay over a white muslin dress with a deep border of embroidery and black lace, both shot through with silver thread. Short full sleeves made of the crepe were trimmed with the same lace at the cuffs. The modiste had declared the dress to be a beautiful addition to her wardrobe and perfect for the mourning period. "I laid your matching gloves and slippers in the chair."

Once Evie had dressed, the maid arranged her hair.

"I think the beaded pins would be pretty," she said, securing them around her soft cascade of golden blonde braids. The maid stepped back and admired her work. "I think you look lovely. Now be off with you while I take your cat and her brood to the kitchen for their sustenance. I think she needs some proper nourishment."

Alice left, carrying the basket full of felines. Keeping them together was the easiest way to move them. She did not trust the kittens not to scurry throughout the house.

Evie took a last look in the mirror before she hurried downstairs.

Winters met her at the base of the stairs. "My lady, His Grace is waiting in the parlor." He accompanied her to the parlor and opened the door.

Adam stood at the window with his back to her. He slowly turned. She noted appreciatively how the morning sun stressed his broad shoulders and muscular legs. Evie observed that Winters had left the door open. *Alice should be here at any moment.*

"Lady Evie, you are a vision," Adam said, stepping away from the window. He took her gloved hand and kissed the top. "The deep purple is a perfect color for your eyes."

Warmth shot to her core. Since "the rescue," Adam had paid her nonstop attention, seeing her almost every day. "Good morning, Adam," she replied, smiling. "I had not expected you to call this morning. This is a pleasant surprise." She gazed up at him, admiring his strong jawline and aquiline nose. His longish brown hair hid the scar on the side of his face. However, to her eye, the thin, jagged scar enhanced his handsome features and disappeared when he smiled. Unable to resist, she raised her hand and ran it softly over it. She felt him stiffen and look away beneath her touch.

"Adam, I apologize. I should not have behaved with such familiarity," she fretted.

When he looked up at her, his eyes had darkened with pain.

"Were you injured at Waterloo?" Her words were soft.

"No, nothing quite that honorable." He took a deep breath. "I should tell you the truth. I became injured in a duel—it had ended, or so I thought. However, the man who lost cheated. When Willington warned me, I turned to defend myself, and his sword sliced my face."

She drew in her breath, steadying herself. "That is horrible," she answered. "I fear you believe it repulses me," she mumbled, now painfully aware that Alice could walk in upon them. She could not understand what was taking Alice so long.

His hands cupped her face, and he looked at her.

His touch sent shivers down her arms and into her very core. For a long moment, she studied him. "I find you attractive, Adam, as I always have." She could feel a furious blush stealing up her face as she spoke.

"You find me *appealing?"*

"I do," she said softly. Competing emotions of adoration and embarrassment swirled throughout as she struggled for the right words. "Your scar reminds me of the honorable man I know you to be. I am content not to know the details..."

"I killed him," he interrupted, "and I should make this known to you. It was Lord Aster."

"Oh. I see," she stammered and became silent. *Of course he would avenge Honora.*

"Evie, I tell you all of this, not because of Honora—I fear that is what you think. Rather, it is because of how I feel for you. I have never felt this level of attraction before. We spend one day together, and I look forward to the next…and the next. My feelings for Honora were never thus. Once I avenged her death, I felt guilt for *not* thinking of her. Yet I am consumed with thoughts of you," he said, his voice laden with emotion.

She met his eyes. "I also look forward to time with you. I confess that the sleigh ride was hard to top; however, racing our horses this the day before yesterday was great fun. I won, by the way," she teased, then peered up at him, her gaze stopping at his mouth.

A smile lit his face. "Only because you took that shortcut across the stream. It was dangerous. Your horse could have slipped."

"You exaggerate. My horse has done that many times," she murmured.

"Not on ice," he breathed and edged his face closer to hers.

"You are being a terrible loser," she uttered, her gaze locked on his lips.

"I want to kiss you," he whispered. He pulled her closer, and his breath gently fanned against her temple.

She pushed up onto her tiptoes and closed her eyes, waiting.

His lips covered hers, while his tongue teased the opening of her mouth, urging her to open for him. She adored his kisses.

Heavens. Thank goodness Alice had not walked in on that. They would force poor Adam to marry—

"Ahem." He cleared his throat, interrupting her thoughts.

"I have a question to ask, and I fear there will never be a better moment." He kissed her temple and brushed a kiss on her lips before pulling back. Taking a small step backward, he closed the door with his foot.

Evie nervously sucked in her breath, and her heart began pounding in her ears. Alice said he had spoken to Papa. Was this truly happening? Her eyes misted, and tears ebbed unchecked.

Adam dropped to one knee. His eyes searched hers. "Lady Evie Roberts, will you do me the honor of becoming my duchess? I have never been in love before. However, when I am near you, it feels like home to me. You see beyond my imperfect face. My heart tells me that what we have *is* love. I never thought I would find it, yet it has always been here—always with you."

"Y-yes! I will marry you." Evie struggled to find her voice.

"Now, I think we should continue that kiss," he said, picking her up and covering her lips with his own.

A few minutes later, a knock sounded, and the door opened. Father, Alice, and Winters stood in the threshold.

"I take it by the grins on both yer faces, 'tis safe to enter and congratulate ye both," Alice pronounced with a smirk.

"Let me be the first to welcome you to the family, son," the earl said, grinning from ear to ear.

"I hope you do not mind my offering congratulations, Your Grace. I have known Lady Evie since she was a baby and am happy to see her settled with a good man," said the old retainer.

The blush that stole up her face when the door opened felt almost permanent.

"Any idea of when you plan to get married?" her father asked. "I think your father would want you to go with your hearts' desire."

Adam put his hand in his pocket. "I hope that you will not think me hasty, but I wanted you to have your choice of days, including Christmastide. I secured a special license." He turned to Evie. "Do you have a special day in mind, my love?"

Evie's heart squeezed. Had he called her his love?

"If you two have not made plans for today, I was wondering if you could help me deliver baskets to my tenants. Cook has them made up, but I am afraid that with the extraordinary snow we have gotten, it could take me twice as long," Papa suggested, with a grin. "I know you both did this yesterday on your estate, Adam, but I would be most appreciative."

"I am more than willing. What about you, Evie?" Adam suggested.

"That would be marvelous fun, Papa. I will remember my muff and the right pelisse this time too," she added, laughing.

Handing out gifts of food, cloth, and candy for the children had been enjoyable with Adam. Her father went to a lot of trouble each year to make sure he gave acceptable gifts to their tenants. Splitting the gift baskets up for delivery made so much sense in this weather and the offerings were appreciated by every tenant. The children enjoyed the hard candies and the little cakes that had been included. Cook had gone with Papa, and they had all returned at almost the same time.

When they pulled into the drive, Adam leaned over and pulled her to him. "You will make a wonderful duchess, Evie." He kissed her deeply. "I think I must have always loved you. I did not realize the depth of my feelings until recently."

"Mmm. I like your kisses," she murmured, not wanting to open her eyes and break the spell she was under.

He lightly chucked her chin. "I think I should be on my way home. I need to dress and gather Mother and Beatrice for tonight's dinner."

"You are right." She sighed. "Do they know?"

"They do." He smiled. "And it thrills them. Can you imagine how hard it would be to keep a secret from my mother?"

"I suppose not. She knows her son," Evie agreed as he helped her down from his carriage.

"I need one more kiss…just to tide me over," she said, pulling his face to hers and covering his lips with her own.

EPILOGUE

Twelfth Night
6 January 1816

A knock sounded at the door, and her father stuck his head into the room. "Mind if I enter? Alice indicated you were dressed."

"Papa. I was just standing here thinking about how my life had changed in what seems like an instant."

"It has," he agreed. "However, I wish you happy, and that is part of why I came here." He held out a folded piece of vellum.

She looked into his eyes and noticed tears had formed. "What is it, Papa?"

"It is from your mother." He heaved a sigh and sat on the edge of her bed, patting the cover for her to sit next to him.

The edge of her bed had been the place where she and her father had most of their serious conversations.

"Your mother wrote it when she realized she would not be with you for the major events of your life. She was a strong woman, just as you are. Had influenza not taken her..." His voice lowered to a whisper.

"Shall I open it?" Her simple question brought a smile to his face.

"By all means. I have held it for years, wondering what she wrote to you. She asked me to give it to you the day you married. That would be today." He chuckled.

She looked at it for a long moment before she took her finger and guided it beneath the seal, breaking it. A tear escaped, and she wiped it away as she carefully opened her letter.

My darling Evie,

It is your wedding day! I would have loved to be there and share in your day. However, I have never been far from you or your father. With your father's encouragement, I feel sure you have grown into a lovely young woman with the gentlest of hearts, along with a good dose of independence. I am smiling as I write this. You are surely the best of both of us, my sweet daughter.

I asked your father to pass my pearl and emerald necklace to you. If it matches your dress, please wear it. The necklace is delicate and beautiful. I wore it on my wedding day. It was a gift from your father.
I love you, Evie. Embrace your new adventure and your new life. Here is the advice I would have given you.

Marriage is the most wonderful of life's gifts, especially when founded in love. Treasure each other, be honest, and do not go to bed angry.

All my love,
Mother

Her father laid a black velvet box in her lap. "It was your mother's. She asked that I give this to you on your wedding day."

Evie opened it gingerly and recognized the strand immediately as one her mother wore frequently, although she had never known its significance.

"Can you help me put it on, Papa?" She turned and allowed her father to secure the necklace.

"It matches your dress beautifully, child."

She had had her mother's dress refashioned into a style for the present day. A shimmering white crepe overlay hung over a satin slip that hinted at the barest color of green, tastefully ornamented with silver and green thread. Her turban headdress was made of white crepe and decorated with matching thread. The modiste had worked extra hard to get it ready for the wedding. She would carry a small bouquet of white roses with sprigs of evergreen. Everything was perfect. Her mother's letter and necklace made her feel she would also be in attendance. That thought warmed her heart. She missed her mother terribly.

"Is it time to go?" she asked.

"I think so," Papa replied. "Alice is probably chafing at the bit. Cook will make sure the wedding breakfast is perfect."

The small party of three rode quietly to the chapel, an elegant stone church that had been in the family for generations and had witnessed many of the family weddings. Several horses and two carriages with the Lancaster crest sat outside. The scenery looked like a beautiful painting that her mother would have loved. Trees that looked almost sugar coated and a carpet of glistening snow made the landscape almost perfect. When she entered the chapel, she realized that Alice had outdone herself with decorations of roses, holly, and evergreens. The candlelight made it all stunning. She wanted to pinch herself to make sure this was no dream.

Their wedding stayed a simple affair. When the vicar asked to bless the ring, Adam handed him a small blue velvet pouch. The cleric opened the pouch and extracted a delicate stack of golden bands, each with a different colored stone, secured tightly together into one beautiful band. He blessed the ring, and with a slight wave of his hand, indicated it was time to place the ring on her finger.

Adam turned to her and took her hands. He lifted her right hand and kissed it. "Evie, this band of rings has been part of my family for generations, designed for the women who would become duchess. My father passed these to me." Pointing out each intricate band one by one, he explained them before placing them on her finger. "Each band symbolizes the special moments in the discovery of our love. This gold band engraved with tiny flowers symbolizes the moment of first notice." He looked at her. "I think that was at my father's funeral."

Evie felt the tears begin to well in her eyes.

"This one with the embedded ruby made to appear as part of a small engraved flower on a single vine commemorates our first kiss. The third one with the small sapphire implanted in the flower vine symbolizes the moment I realized how much you mattered to me."

"When was that?" she whispered.

"When I first realized you were missing, it took all the effort I had to just breathe," he admitted, his voice low. "The small emerald embedded in a flower vine represents our engagement," he said fingering the fourth band. "And this fifth band of gold with delicate etchings of two flowers wrapped around an embedded diamond stands for today, our wedding day," he said, sliding the intricately banded ring on her finger. "If you hold it just right," he demonstrated, "the vine appears to wrap continuously around your finger."

A single tear rolled down her cheek when he placed the ring on her finger. "Thank you, Adam. This is something I never expected. It is truly beautiful."

After a moment, the vicar cleared his throat. "I confess, I have never seen one so beautiful," he whispered. And louder, he said, "I now pronounce you man and wife." The couple turned to face their families and closest friends. "May I introduce the Duke and Duchess of Lancaster?"

Amid hearty congratulations and warm hugs and kisses, the couple made it to their carriage.

"I have a surprise, dear wife," Adam offered once they were inside the vehicle.

"I love your surprises, husband." She laughed. "Just a guess, but I believe everyone knows about this surprise except me."

"Why do you say that?"

"Because they are all waving us off, which I find unusual. Then there was that gleam in my father's eyes. I cannot recall seeing him this happy in years—not since my mother's passing," she responded, smiling.

"Ah. You have to wait." He knocked on the roof, and the coach lurched forward.

About twenty minutes later, they pulled up in front of her mother's small cabin. Smoke was coming from the chimney. Greenery was edged around the windows, and there was a fresh coat of white paint. It was beautiful.

He gently lifted her from the carriage and carried her into the cottage where the smell of fresh baked bread wafted. She gasped. It was beautiful. When they closed the door, she heard the coach leave.

"He will return tomorrow for us," Adam said. "What do you think?" He waved his hand at the room before them.

The small chaise longue had been replaced with a larger bed, and they had turned the room into a small honeymoon cottage. Warm, colorful carpets covered the floors, and several of her mother's paintings hung tastefully on the walls. Toward the back of the room, a small table readied with plates sat next to another side table covered with food—meats, cheeses, fresh breads, and fruits.

"This is beautiful. I never imagined such a place. Will they not be looking for us to share the breakfast?"

"Do not worry about that. My mother and your father have things well in hand." He lifted the strand of emeralds and pearls from her neck with his finger. "Come here, wife. We have much to do, and I feel a sense of urgency to start some of it now," he said with a low voice. "This time, there will be no need to rescue you from the cabin." He cupped her face and pulled her close.

Standing on her tiptoes, she twirled her hands in his hair. "I have everything I ever could have imagined. I have married my love."

"I love you, Evie. Never doubt my love for you," he said, pulling her into his arms. "You have made me the happiest of men."

Please sign up for my newsletter for new release info, interesting research updates, contests & more! https://www.annastclaire.com

ALSO BY ANNA ST. CLAIRE

Earl of Weston

Earl of Bergen

Earl of Shefford

Lyon's Prey

The Earl She Left Behind

Romancing A Wallflower

Embers of Anger

Wicked Earls Christmas

O Night Divine : A Holiday Collection of Spirited Christmas Tales

Hello Rogue

'Twas A Rogue Before Christmas

ACKNOWLEDGMENTS

There are always so many people to thank when a book gets written. First, my friends who always cheer me on...Elizabeth Johns, Lauren Smith, Myra Platt, Betty Phillips, and Jessica Cale.

A great big thank you goes to my team of readers who spent time and gave up evenings to help me smooth out the rough edges. Thank you, Pat, Lori, Theresa, and Aunt Tricia.

ABOUT THE AUTHOR

Anna St. Claire is a big believer that *nothing* is impossible if you believe in yourself. She sprinkles her stories with laughter, romance, mystery and lots of possibilities, adhering to the belief that goodness and love will win the day.

Anna is both an avid reader author of American and British historical romance. She and her husband live in Charlotte, North Carolina with their two dogs and often, their two beautiful granddaughters, who live nearby. *Daughter, sister, wife, mother, and Mimi*—all life roles that Anna St. Claire relishes and feels blessed to still enjoy. And she loves her pets – dogs and cats alike, and often inserts them into her books as secondary characters. And she loves chocolate and popcorn, a definite nod to her need for sweet followed by salty...*but not together*—a tasty weakness!

Anna relocated from New York to the Carolinas as a child. Her mother, a retired English and History teacher, always encouraged Anna's interest in writing, after discovering short stories she would write in her spare time.

As a child, she loved mysteries and checked out every *Encyclopedia Brown* story that came into the school library. Before too long, her fascination with history and reading led her to her first historical romance—Margaret Mitchell's *Gone With The Wind*, now a treasured, but weathered book from being read multiple times. The day she discovered Kathleen Woodiwiss,' books, *Shanna* and *Ashes In The Wind*, Anna became hooked. She read every historical romance that came her way and dreams of writing her own historical romances took seed.

Today, her focus is primarily the Regency and Civil War eras, although Anna enjoys almost any period in American and British history. She would love to connect with any of her readers on her website – www.annastclaire.com, through email—annastclaireauthor@gmail.com, Instagram – annastclaire_author, BookBub – www.bookbub.com/profile/anna-st-claire,Twitter – @1AnnaStClaire, Facebook – https://www.facebook.com/authorannastclaire/ or on Amazon – https://www.amazon.com/Anna-St-Claire/e/B078WMRHHF?ref=.

NOBLE
HEARTS
THE
EARL
SHE LEFT
BEHIND
ANNA ST. CLAIRE

THE EARL SHE LEFT BEHIND

BY ANNA ST. CLAIRE

Chapter One

Maidstone, Kent, England

October 1815

Thunder boomed above him. A second later, a sharp crack of lightning lit up the dark sky. Gripping the reins of his horse, Maxwell Wilde, Earl of Worsley, fought to stay seated as his mare reared and struggled. The lightning illuminated a woman lying in the road just ahead. Had the lightning not struck, he most certainly would not have seen her.

The scant light showed a small-framed woman curled into a fetal position, wearing a soiled blue dress. A small shaggy white dog pawed her arm, whimpering and licking her face. Large drops of rain pelted both of them but did not affect the dog's loyal persistence.

"Whoa, Willow." Max slid from his mount and walked over to the woman. At his approach, the dog at once became protective, giving a guttural growl. It forced Max to stop and rethink his goal.

"Easy, boy." He lowered his hand to the dog and allowed him to sniff it. The dog stopped growling and eased himself down, curling his furry white body next to the woman's head —protecting her—still whimpering and licking her face. Max took a deep breath, careful not to anger the dog and not wanting to injure it. The dog was unmistakably attached to the woman. Feeling more confident the dog would not attack him, he lowered himself onto his haunches to get a better look at the woman.

Gently, he swept wet, muddied blonde tresses from her face. Recognition was swift and tumultuous. "Bloody hell! Meg, what happened? Why are you out in this storm, of all places? Why are you here?" Questions flooded his brain. He fought the gut-wrenching impulse to pull her close. When she did not answer, he picked up a limp hand and noticed rope burns around her left wrist, anger registering. "You are bleeding." He moved her damp blonde hair away from her forehead, revealing a deep gash from which blood still oozed. Fear gripped him. He stared at her motionless body until he saw her chest barely move. Good. She was breathing. "Thank goodness you are still alive."

Her eyes opened and closed. Her throat worked, but she did not speak. She needed a doctor. Max needed to get her to safety and leave before she engaged his heart yet again.

He had washed his hands of Maggie Winters when she ran away and abruptly married the Earl of Tipton three years past—when she and Max were planning to wed. Anger churned in his gut as he thought about the day he found out, and it renewed his confusion, pain, and anger. She had disappeared without a word—merely a scribbled note delivered to him. Without thinking, he reached inside this waistcoat pocket and touched the folded missive. No one had heard from Maggie in years. It was strange, but word of her marriage had cleared it up for him. He squashed the now-familiar feeling of dread.

"No, no, no! Leave him alone! Please...do not harm him." Her voice was hoarse and barely audible. She rolled her head from left to right and moved her hands about herself in defense—defending against what, he did not understand. Was she speaking about the small dog? With one eye on Max, the dog was furiously licking her face. He was trying to calm her. *Amazing.*

The small animal gave a sharp bark, trying to gain her attention. "Rrrr...uff."

Unsure of the dog's reaction to his presence, he increased the space between them. He had no wish to have an animal of any size bite him. But the bark itself triggered an awareness. He vaguely recalled having met this animal. But when? He narrowed his eyes, attempting to remember. It had been a while since he had seen Meg. She could have gained a pet without his notice. It had been three years since he had last laid eyes on her.

The heaviness in his heart was returning. Max had tried to forget her. He wanted to forget her. The last thing he needed was to be in her presence now. But Meg's condition terrified him. Ignoring her was not an option. He smoothed the wet hair away from the sides of her face.

Lifting her, he placed her on his saddle. Her body slumped. He leaned in close, holding her against his shoulder, then put his left foot in the stirrup and hoisted himself up behind her. He held her gently in case there was any other injury he had not seen. The touch of her sent his pulse racing, but Max did his best to hold on to Meg and the reins. The dog started barking and jumping, almost bouncing, desperate to gain access to his mistress. Willow twisted and bared her teeth at the dog, as if to tell him to stop, but the small animal was unfazed. He would have to bring the dog.

This dog means something to Meg. Recognition almost knocked him out of his seat. This bedraggled white dog was the same grubby puppy they had saved moments before an out-of-control wagon and its horses would have ended its life, only weeks before Meg had disappeared from his. His heart sped with excitement that she had kept it all this time. "I know you!" He looked down at the dog. "It is coming back to me now." Excited, he leaned into Meg. "I recognize Shep. You kept the dog!" he whispered, realizing she would not hear him but needing to speak. Overwhelmed, he pulled her tight to his chest and breathed in her essence. Lilacs. His favorite. He loved that she always smelled of lilacs. Once upon a time, she told him it was her preferred flower.

The dog waited. Its demeanor communicated the anticipation of accommodation. "I will not leave you. Give me a moment to think." He was speaking almost to himself. It was a difficult position. Thinking rapidly, he reached behind him for his saddlebag and emptied its contents. Nothing of importance was in there. Once satisfied with the space, he carefully slid off his horse, keeping one hand holding onto Meg. She did not move. Hurriedly, he gathered the small dog into the satchel. Shep gave no resistance. Max hoisted the bags over his shoulder to allow the small dog to ride, and once again mounted Willow.

"Shep," she murmured, barely conscious. Her voice was weak. "Shep, where are you?" She tried to open her eyes, but they fluttered closed again.

A lighter bark registered under his arm. He could not believe his ears. The dog had answered her. It *understood* her.

Willow turned into Max's estate and stopped at the front. It had been six months since his last visit home. Still securing Meg with one hand, he slid from his horse, and lowered his saddlebag, allowing the dog to leave it. Then he turned back and gently helped Meg down.

"Follow me." He nodded at the dog, confident the pooch understood him. Holding Meg in his arms, he and the bedraggled pup made it up the steps to the portico and pushed open the door.

The slow but pronounced footfalls of his butler sounded a welcome.

"Your lordship, you have returned. We had not expected you this evening." The tall, greying man drew closer and peered down at the drenched woman in his arms. "I apologize for ogling, my lord, but that is Miss Maggie...pardon, *Lady* Maggie..." He looked up at Max. "Lady Tipton." Max noted the shock and concern in the old man's eyes. "She appears injured. What happened, my lord?" Before Max could answer, the older man noticed the small dog standing at Max's feet and scowled. "Shoo! Out the door with you."

Shep sprung into the air, jumping vertically toward his mistress and barking his high-pitched bark. The energy the dog still had despite the frigid conditions he had endured astonished Max. "It's okay, Cabot. Lady..." He paused, grappling for words. "Lady Tipton needs the dog as much as he needs her. He stays."

"As you wish, my lord. I will send for the doctor." His displeasure clear, Cabot left the room, but not before giving a quick glare toward the dog.

"Thank you, Cabot," he responded under his breath to the man's back. Louder, he added, "Send for Mrs. Andrews and have her meet me upstairs. I shall put Lady...Tipton in Lady Angela's room." Uttering her married name renewed the ache in his chest. He needed to get her help and then distance himself. Angela, his sister, would not mind Meg using her room while she visited her best friend in London. Angela would be gone for at least two more weeks.

It would not be easy to forget Meg's marriage status with three years past, but he had to for his sanity. And he needed to stop calling her Meg. That had been his nickname for her. She was Lady Maggie Tipton now. Even as he told himself this, he knew it would be impossible—she would always be Meg to him.

Meg's body quaked, probably from the chill. Responding on impulse, Max pulled her closer, hoping to share his body warmth in the only way he knew. She was lighter than he recalled. Her lilac scent rushed his senses and reminded him sharply of his loss. Weirdly, he recalled a time or two he had carried her. Rapt in the past, he missed a step, barely catching himself before he lost his balance.

"Woof!" The dog ran past him up the stairs and stopped at the top. He watched Max the rest of the way up, his expression one of mistrust.

"I promise not to hurt her." *No, I will be the one in pain here,* Max reflected. "It is just ahead, Shep." Good God! He was talking to a dog. Shaking off the realization, he nodded toward the hall. Shep started in behind him, following him into the room. Once inside, Max laid Meg on the pink velvet-covered bed.

Shep jumped up and sniffed at her face, assuring himself she was still alive. Once satisfied, he inspected each of the four large posters before curling up next to her side. Not close enough, his little body edged toward her until it touched her.

"Shep, you have come back," she uttered, weakly placing her hand on his folded front paws with a loud sigh.

Was that relief? His gaze shifted to the burns on her wrists, and he knew he could not dismiss her again from his life so quickly. *I need to know what happened to her.* The burns on Meg's wrists bothered him as much as her tortured state of mind. Was she running from someone...or maybe *to* something? Whatever it was, the dog had a part in it. He had found her in front of her family's estate. Wyndham was almost a mile from his own property.

He had planned to ask for her hand, but a carriage accident claimed the lives of both of her parents the very day he had planned to see her father. Everyone had expected them to marry—he had made his feelings about Maggie clear. He loved her and thought the feeling was mutual. But two days after the funeral for her parents, Maggie Winters had disappeared, leaving only the note.

Her uncle, Silas Winters, had become her guardian, inheriting her father's title of viscount and his entitled properties. Max knew Silas for his gambling and questionable business dealings. Meg had been most unhappy to learn he was to be her guardian until she turned one and twenty.

Wyndham had been her mother's childhood home, but the Winters family had lived there most of the time. Following the death of his brother, Viscount Silas Winters had boarded up the property, never sending a soul to care for it. Max's mother had written that recent sightings of a woman in white staring from the attic window had renewed the rumor that the estate was haunted.

He took a deep breath and gazed at the sleeping woman in front of him. Three years had passed. Max had buried her memory, pushing it to the back of his mind, but seeing her tonight, holding her, and smelling her essence brought painful memories of his loss to the forefront. He had met with her uncle to ask for her hand, and the contracts were being drawn up when Maggie Winters had left town, suddenly marrying a much older Fergus Anders, Earl of Tipton. She had left Max's life with no explanation. Cornered, her uncle would only say he had signed a contract. Nothing more. Max felt he would never know the truth, only the note she left him. The rumors, which were hard to believe, only added salt to his wounded heart.

The gossip was that Meg's uncle had married her to Tipton to settle a gambling loss. Both were notorious gamblers, and the thought that Meg had been taken away unwillingly only added deeper angst. Max had never been sure of what had happened, but he could not reach her, despite his best efforts. With no contract signed, he had no chance of winning her back—if that had even been what had happened. He had heard nothing from her. The loss had decimated Max's heart. He had sworn to never love again, but now he realized he had never stopped loving her. He left town shortly after she did, not willing or able to endure the pity of being jilted by the one person he loved more than life itself.

I can never let her know my feelings.

Max shook his head, hoping to pull himself from his misery. *She is Tipton's wife, yet she is here. Why?* He pulled up one of his sister's pink velvet slipper chairs and sat next to her. "Meg, why are you here now? What happened to you?" The dog opened his eyes and stared at him, never lifting his head. A low, guttural growl erupted.

"I will not hurt her." Max reached tentatively and stroked the cotton-soft hair on the dog's head. Shep allowed it and sniffed his hand. A slight wag of his tail replaced the growl. *Good. He recognizes me.* "Good boy."

Meg's quick wit and sense of adventure had been something he always enjoyed. They got along better together than his school friends, and he had continually enjoyed coming home to her. There was always one scrape or another, and he was always rescuing her—until he could not.

Female voices and the swishing of skirts drew his attention to the door as his mother entered.

"My dear, Cabot mentioned that you had brought Lady

Tipton in from an accident. I quickly allowed my guests to leave and came to help." She looked at the prone form in her daughter's bed. "I had to see for myself."

"Mother, thank you. I had not realized you would be here. I thought you were in London for the Season. I am sorry about your guests, but…" He glanced down at Meg. "I found her like this on my way home. She was in front of her parents' gate. With the dog." He nodded at Shep. "That is the dog Meg and I found shortly before…" He took a deep breath. "Shortly before we were to be wed."

"I recall that incident. You could have both died saving the rascal." She smiled at that dog. "I rarely allow dogs in my home, but he seems harmless. I will plan for a bath and some food for him." She sniffed in Shep's direction. "Immediately."

"Lord Worsley, the doctor should be here in a few minutes. Cabot sent the footman for him straightaway." Mrs. Andrews tapped him lightly on the arm.

"Son, I will take over. You change out of those wet clothes." His mother placed her hands on his shoulders and squeezed lightly.

Nodding, Max agreed. "I shall change and be right back." His hand lightly grazed Maggie's. "It would be best not to move her further until the doctor examines her. She has burns on her wrists, and I am most concerned there could be hidden injuries."

"My God! She does." His mother said, her tone one of alarm as she gently rolled Maggie's wrist and leaned in to look more closely. "They appear to be rope burns. Who would have placed ropes on Maggie?"

Shep lifted his head and started to growl, but a sharp, reproachful look from his mother squelched that. Max swallowed a chuckle as he started to leave.

"It is Shep, is it not?" His mother's inquiry stopped him.

"Yes. You recall that? I almost did not recognize him. He

is a protective little chap." He walked over and ruffled the dog's head affectionately.

"I do." She smiled. "I confess, these last three years, I have had a hard time thinking of her as Lady Tipton. She was to be my daughter, but she has not been part of society. I just can't imagine..." Her voice trailed off as her hand gently moved a little wet and bloodied hair from Meg's face. "Something drastic has happened. We shall help her all we can."

Max paused a moment to regard the bedraggled woman he had just placed in his sister's bed. Her eyes were shuttered closed. Thick dark lashes brushed the tops of her cheekbones in their resting state. Long blonde hair framed her face and covered her shoulders. Even wet, the color reminded him of sunshine and yellow roses. She was beautiful. His traitorous arms ached to hold her, to comfort her, but he would not.

She is married, he reminded himself. Max's gaze held her sleeping form a moment longer before he again noticed the angry red abrasions on her wrists. His body stiffened in anger. *Mother is right. I need time to regroup my thoughts.*

"Thank you, Mother." He stopped just before leaving the room and turned back. "The dog..." He paused and looked at the white bundle of fur curled up next to Maggie. "I must allow Shep to stay here with her. Please make sure the doctor tries to accommodate. She keeps reaching for him. I fear that whatever has transpired, Shep may be Meg's only witness and her biggest comfort."

THE EARL SHE LEFT BEHIND

— CLICK HERE TO READ THE REST!

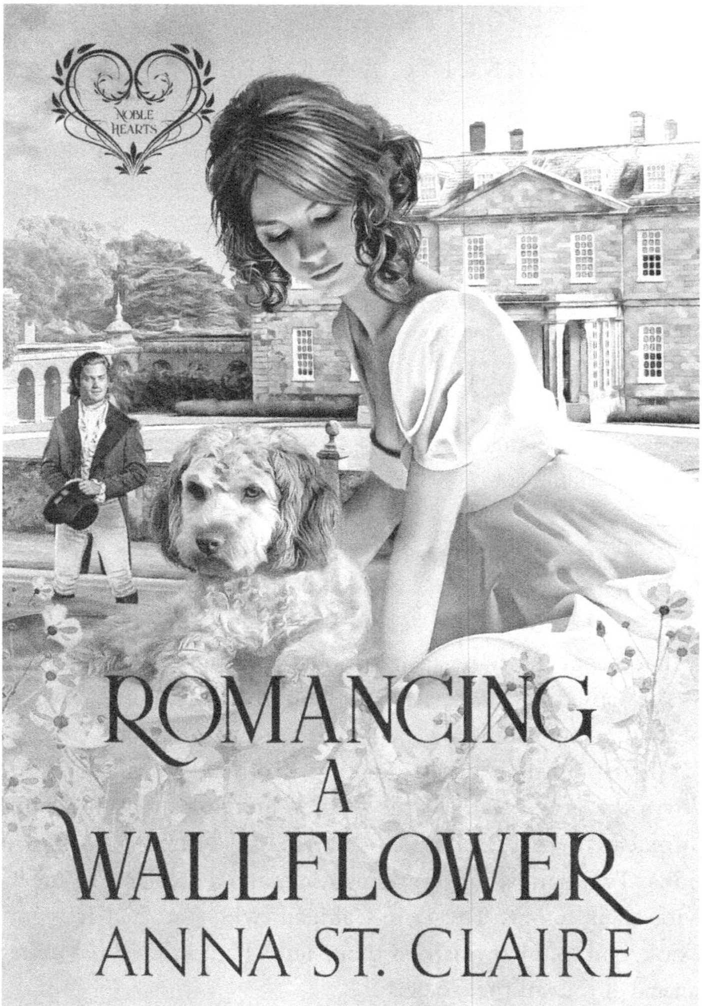
NOBLE HEARTS
ROMANCING A WALLFLOWER
ANNA ST. CLAIRE

ROMANCING A WALLFLOWER

BY ANNA ST. CLAIRE

Prologue

August 1815

Tintagel, England

"That was a narrow escape! I thought Chambers was going to tell us Mama was looking for us." Lydia DeLacey put her hand to her mouth, smothering her giggles as she joined her twin sister at the bottom of the front steps of their father's house.

"Hurry!" Lilian urged. Picking up their skirts, they ran down the gravel path to the stables, arriving breathless and intoxicated with excitement at avoiding Mama's machinations. Two handsome gentlemen had arrived earlier to meet with their father. The twin's abigail, who had had it from Cook, had told her mistress that Mama had ordered tea to be served at four of the clock.

Lilian hated to think her father would arrange marriages for her sister and herself—not when he and their mother still enjoyed a love match. However, her mother was notorious for *creating opportunities,* as she termed it, for her two daughters to meet the men of their dreams and seemed determined, despite Lilian and her twin showing no interest in any of their suitors, to find at least one match.

Her joyous mood changed when she saw the head groom waiting at the door of the stables.

"Oh, marvellous! Barney is waiting for us," she muttered with a hint of sarcasm.

"We will have to take him, Lilian."

She yearned to ride Danby, the dark bay she had brought on from birth. She loved the fresh air and thrilled to the independence riding her horse gave her. Often, she and Lydia rode neck and neck, racing over the pastures and fields of her parent's estate. Such freedom was impossible in London.

"Good morning, my lady and my lady." Barney, the head groom, stepped forward with their horses. "I took the liberty of having Danby and Ginger saddled. I thought you would wish to ride this morning. Me own horse is also ready." He sent an imploring look in their direction.

Lilian glanced at her sister and then around her, struggling to find an excuse to leave him behind. There was none, although on many an occasion she and her sister had contrived to lose him. The poor man knew they were likely to put him through his paces.

"Thank you, Barney." Lilian smiled tightly. "It is a beautiful day for a ride, is it not? We will endeavour not to trouble you unduly."

"Yes, my lady." He noticeably gulped and led Lydia's horse to the mounting block. He helped each of them onto their horse and climbed upon his own. The small party rode out of the stable yard, Lilian and her sister in the lead and the groom trailing a safe distance behind.

Flowers were in bloom everywhere. A purple blanket of

creeping thyme edged the path. Bluebells and bright yellow cat's ear carpeted the sides of the hill, dominating small sunny areas as it climbed a ridge beyond them, making the small pockets of pink wild roses very noticeable.

"This is truly lovely, Lil. The air even feels cooler. It is perfect weather for our ride," Lydia commented.

"Would you care to ride to the cliffs today?" Lilian questioned.

"I would love to, but do you think we should? Father has asked us to stay close to the house. He does not want us near the cliffs unchaperoned because of the free traders. I do not think he would consider Barney sufficient protection."

Lilian did not care to bear Father's wrath. He was normally a gentle soul, but when it was needful, he could become intractable.

She agreed with her sister. "Yes, the thought of Barney defending our honour is almost too much to contemplate. Very well. What about the ruins? We could follow the ridge and mayhap stretch the horses there."

"That is a good plan. Mama will be so cross! I wonder who these gentlemen are?"

"An earl and his friend, Father said this morning. You were too busy eyeing that new footman to notice."

"Perhaps we should have taken the Season more seriously and she would not be so frantic about our finding suitable matches," Lydia replied. The family had arrived home from London only a week ago and had barely unpacked.

Lilian sighed. "There *was* one gentleman..."

"Oh, I know the one you mean, and I noticed *your* reaction to him. He was wearing his regimental dress although, according to Mama, he is an earl."

Lilian was not surprised Lydia knew exactly the man she remembered. It had been the last ball of the Season. She drew in a breath, recalling how she had noticed him the moment he had entered the room.

"I will admit I wished he would ask me to dance, but he and his friend did not seem to remain long."

"Quite. I noticed him watching you and thought he would ask to be introduced, but then his friend came back with glasses of champagne, said something to him and they left."

"Perhaps there was an emergency." Her mind flitted back to that night. "They were both interesting, but so were several others. I noticed you seemed taken with Viscount Yarstone." Although she spoke the words, Lilian's mind was still on the gentleman in the regimentals.

"Do come down from the clouds, sister," Lydia teased.

Wrinkling her nose at Lydia, Lilian gave her horse a slight nudge, sending him into a canter. Her hat came off and she felt her hair fall from its pins until her long auburn brown curls were flowing behind her. She did not care. She had Danby, and she was here on this glorious morning. It was all that mattered.

Her sister looked behind them. "Good heavens! Barney is keeping up!" Immodestly, Lydia yelled across the space between them, gesturing with a jerk of her head and obviously goading Lilian to look.

Instead, Lilian sniggered in a rude way and gave Danby another nudge. Her brown gelding ran faster, forcing Lydia and her chestnut to race to catch them. It felt wondrous. The two sisters rode across the crest of the hill for a good while, deftly dodging trees, fences and outcrops of rock—doggedly followed, some distance behind, by their groom. Low shrubs and weathered post-and-rail fencing bordered one edge of the path they followed, and masses of coloured flowers covered the ground, gradually disappearing from sight.

A more wooded area appeared in a bend in the track ahead of them, and as they approached, a loud shot rang out.

Danby shied violently sideways and with a shrill squeal of distress, reared high on his back legs.

"Lilian!" Lydia cried out.

Lilian heard her sister's cry and was dimly aware of her struggles to gain control over Ginger, but her own struggle to maintain her seat was failing. Somehow, her legs loosened from the pommels of her side-saddle when the horse rose, and she fought to keep her balance. Danby lost his footing and as he toppled, the force of him hitting the earth tossed her to the ground. She landed on a stone, or something equally hard, the momentum then rolling her across the rough ground until she thudded into a large rock. She heard her own scream pierce the air.

Lydia and the groom tried to lift her, but she screamed in pain at their touch. Although she could see them speaking to her, their voices sounded distant. Her vision was growing darker and she could barely see; she was viewing their faces and the sky behind them through a small, dark hole which kept shrinking. Her world was growing dark. Her head and her back ached fiercely. Her ears were ringing. She wanted to scream and tried yet could hear nothing. Pain throbbed from every part of her body. She tried to move, to get up, but her feet...*what was wrong with her feet?* They were not moving. What had she done? Her head pounded, and warm liquid ran down the side of her face. A large warm hand grasped hers and at last she heard voices.

"Lady Lilian, can you hear me?"

"Lilian, please speak to me." Wet drops hit Lilian's face. Her sister was crying, it seemed. Whatever had happened to her, it must be bad.

She tried to open her eyes but could see naught but blackness. *I am so tired.*

"We heard a shot and then saw the horses. We came to help." A strong, masculine voice penetrated the fog in her head. *Who was this?* She could hear only snippets of the conversation because of the ringing in her ears.

"Lady Lilian, we must move you..."

"...gown ripped..."

"...back of gown wet with blood."

Are they talking about me?

Lilian felt herself being lifted and then coming to rest against a warm body. The horse shifted beneath them and was soothed with a soft murmur. She could smell the comforting aroma of its sweat, and shivered. Why was she so cold? She recognized her sister's voice, but her garbled words were disjointed.

A light scent of bay leaf and bergamot teased her nose. Gentlemen's and lady's colognes had been in abundance during her coming out, and had mostly tortured her senses, but this was one she liked. How odd that both scents were conveyed so distinctly. *Nothing was making sense. What was happening?* She felt helpless and trapped, now unable to see or hear, and fought against the urge to cry out. A rich voice above her calmed her trembling, and she found she could breathe. She could not hear what was being said, but the voice was soothing. Exhausted, Lilian leaned her head into the warm body holding her and gave in to the darkness that beckoned.

Romancing A Wallflower

— CLICK HERE TO READ THE REST!

Made in the USA
Monee, IL
18 October 2026

66035056R00069